Plan B

and other
Short Stories in support of the

British Deaf Association

Alison Lingwood

Contents

Foreword

Plan B

Love Letter

Hedge Fund

Opposites Attract

Uncle Maurice's Car

Diamonds are Forever

Fava Beans and a Nice Chianti

Roses Grow on You

What Goes Around, Comice Around

The Blue Shoes

Freddie Flies the Nest

Techno Numpty

Rainbow Bridge

First Love

I Would Walk 500 Miles

Drippy Deluge

Happy Landings

The Tree Feller

Bobby's Birthday

From Darkest Peru

Ben Springer's Story

Going, Going, Gone

It's a Dog's Life

Concorde

The Electric Chair

The Lavender Bed

A Tale of Two Nurses

The Bumps

I Wish I'd looked after me Teeth

Toffee's Tale

Nine Patterned Shirts

Heart of Gold

The Call of the Cereal

Neighbours

A Stitch in Time

Chain Gang

Santa's Shoes

The Heist

Weather, not Seasons

Percy

David's Inheritance

And so to Bed

Acknowledgements

Foreword

Estimates suggest that there are over 150,000 UK users of British Sign Language, over 87,000 of whom are deaf. This figure discounts professionals working in the field.

Amazing strides have been made in raising awareness in recent years, from a bill passed through parliament, recognising British Sign Language as an official language, to the introduction of BSL as a GCSE subject from 2025. The BSL in Our Hands initiative promoted by the British Deaf Association is raising awareness of the issues facing the deaf community.

All proceeds from my five volumes:

The Hairdryer died Today
Mission Accomplished!
Wedding Wings
Oh Crumbs!
Plan B

are donated to the British Deaf Association, to further their work into promotion, education and information about BSL and other ways to support the deaf community. As of Plan B's launch date over £1200 has been donated to the charity. I hope that you will enjoy the stories and spread the word to your family and friends.

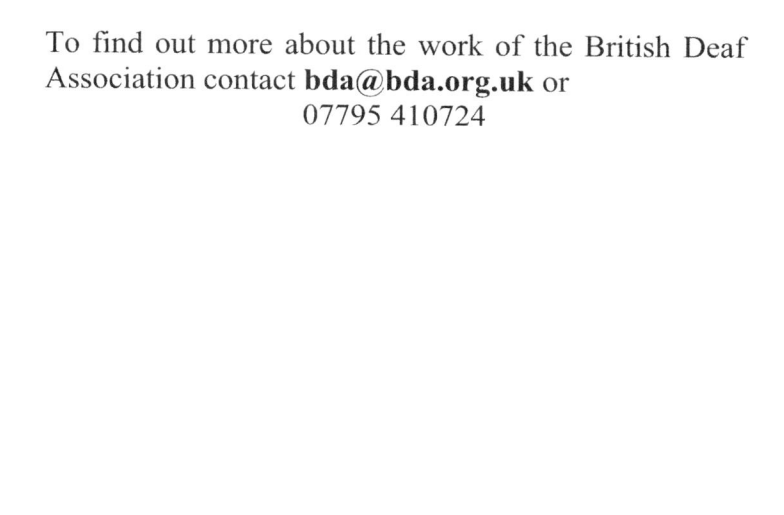

To find out more about the work of the British Deaf Association contact **bda@bda.org.uk** or 07795 410724

Plan B

Colin let out a deep sigh, 'How on earth can the electricity bill be this high in July?' he asked her, 'It's ridiculous.'

'It's not been warm these last few months though, has it Col? I've only had the fan on once, but we have had to use the tumble dryer a fair bit because of the rain. That's all I can think of. Anyway, don't worry about that now. We're going to have a lovely weekend in Reading. Have you put everything you want packing on the bed?'

'Hmmm,' Colin's thoughts were still on the bill, 'We're out at work all week and often not here at the weekends. I'm going to ring the electricity people on Monday. We've been away a fair bit since Christmas; several overnight stays and this just can't be right.'

It was Trish's turn to sigh. 'Col, forget that for

now. We need to get on the road. It's an hour and a half to Oxford, then we can stop for a bite to eat. We'll be in Reading in time to go for a pint with Dennis and Nancy and it'll still be daylight.'

'That'll be nice. It'll be nice to see their new place. You know I'll feel happier arriving in the daylight, with never having driven there before. On Sunday though, if they ask us to stay for an evening meal, I don't mind driving back in the dark. The car would almost find its own way home.'

'Okay,' Trish was business-like, 'Now, I've got the automatic timers out. I thought we'd put one in the kitchen on the radio, and the other on the living room standard lamp, so the light goes off at bedtime as usual. Then with the blinds closed nobody will know that the house is empty for the weekend.'

As the grandfather clock chimed six Trish and Colin were getting in the car and on their way. After a few moments the standard lamp leaned gently over to the window and peeped through the blinds, 'They've gone! Everybody – they've gone. And they won't be back until late on Sunday night. Let's party!'

The grandfather clock cleared his throat, a deep sound that echoed throughout the house.

'Before we all get too excited, we need to think about Sunday. You do realise that we don't know what time they'll be home? Or whether or not they'll be staying for an evening meal even; that was clear from what they said. Normally when they're at work, as you know, I can give you a warning about when they're due back, but not this time, because we just don't know.'

'Ooh - Plan B?' queried the electric fire.

'Plan B,' the clock stated with authority.

The fan, which was fairly new, had heard of Plan B, but never yet experienced it. She became very excited, whirring her blades around at high speed.

''Calm down, Young'un,' said the standard lamp, 'you'll get dizzy, and there's the whole weekend to enjoy first.'

The television clicked on, and the volume turned up as the remote control scrolled through the channels before settling for the loudest it could find. Similarly the radio that had been left on timed burglar duty in the kitchen switched itself on and the dial spun around, changing from the sedate Classic FM to the much more lively Signal FM. The toaster began to shimmy across the kitchen worktop, and from the cupboard, the sound of the kitchen mixer could clearly be heard, whisking away at nothing.

The pendulum on the grandfather clock kept the beat, and Big Len the thermostat turned up the heat, as all the lights switched on and off in a synchronised rhythm throughout the house. The oscillating fan and the standard lamp were dancing together on the rug. From the kitchen the microwave shouted, 'Anybody fancy a warm drink?' and then continued pinging harmoniously, its turntable spinning backwards and forwards. It was a bit subdued when the toaster suggested that perhaps for most of the electrical items plugged into the mains, hot drinks may not be a good idea. So, although the coffee percolator grumbled that the combination of liquid and electricity worked just fine for him, they both just settled back to watch the kettle and toaster dancing together, listening to the music, with the doorbell providing occasional percussive accompaniment.

The television set upstairs in the bedroom was joining in too, but the hairdryer and the iron decided that getting hot in the small spaces where they lived wouldn't be such a good idea, so instead they listened to the radio on the bedside clock.

Knowing that his friend Dennis preferred to wet shave, Colin had packed an ordinary disposable razor for the weekend, much to the delight of his own electric shaver, who was now gyrating to the music along with the extractor fan on the bathroom wall. And so it continued all weekend.

*

It was late and dark on the Sunday evening when suddenly there was a shout from the electric doorbell, whom the others had asked to keep a lookout, 'Quick! They're back!'

'Okay everybody,' boomed the grandfather clock, 'Take your places, you know what you have to do - Plan B!'

Immediately the fuse box in the cupboard in the kitchen flexed his muscles and pressed down as hard as he could until with an audible pop, all the fuses blew. There was absolute silence and all the appliances were immediately still.

No security light turned on as Trish approached the front door, having left Colin to fetch their bags from the car. Once inside she went to flick on the hall light, again and then a third time. Nothing happened. 'Oh no, Colin there's been a power cut. I wonder how long ago that happened. All that food in the freezer! Col, hurry please!'

While Trish panicked about the food, and Colin rummaged in the drawer for a torch, having totally forgotten about the one on his phone, quietly the appliances pressed their buttons and switches, and returned their various dials to where they had previously been set. Under cover of darkness they shuffled back into their original positions. At last Colin found the torch, by which time Trish had crossed to the window.

'The street lights are still on, but next door's in darkness, and the houses opposite. It seems to be very localised. I suppose they might just have gone to bed.'

'Here we go,' Colin said, reaching into the cupboard and flicking the master switch. Immediately the radio on the timer began playing classical music quietly in the kitchen, the standard light came on in the living room, and the freezer began again its gentle hum. The food in the freezer seemed solid enough. From the very brief time lag on the cooker clock they surmised that the power cut must only just have happened and commented on their good luck. Everything else was quiet and still, just as it should be.

And that, Dear Reader, is why there are occasional unexplained power outages. If this happens to you, then remember that one of your near neighbours has undoubtedly been away from home and their appliances have been partying in their absence. And if you've been away yourself, a party at your own house may be the reason why your electricity bill is higher than you expected.

Love Letter

Dear Son,

There's something I always planned to do when the time was right and you met a girl you were serious about and it seems that the time is now. Inside the little packet enclosed with this letter is a ring that you may have seen me wear on special occasions. I wore it as a dress ring, but that isn't quite how it started life.

When your great grandparents – My Nan and Grandad met and decided to marry it was a time when there was little money floating about in the family. The First World War had just ended, many young men were returning from the front looking for work, but jobs were scarce. Jim and Rosa planned to marry but there was no money to spare on non-essentials such as an engagement ring for Rosa. They settled down happily enough and raised the family, my mum, her brother and her sister, and by the time they had been married twenty-five years, only my aunt, who had been a bit of an afterthought, was still living at home. The three children had saved up, and organised a holiday for them to celebrate; nothing too grand but a week in Torquay to them was more luxurious than a cruise would be to us today.

It was while they were in Torquay that Jim said to Rosa that as his anniversary present to her, he would like her to pick out for herself an engagement ring. They still hadn't a lot of money to splash around, but he said later that he took her to a jewellery place in the town. It sounds like it was a pawn shop, as well as a conventional jewellery shop. I remember Rosa put a lot of store by the fact that the ring of her choice was brand new, not a second hand one.

Before Rosa died she gave the ring to me. She told me that she knew I already had an engagement ring, but perhaps I would like to wear hers as a token, as a dress ring, and she was quite right, I was delighted to have it, and I have enjoyed wearing it for twenty years, but the time is ripe now for it to move on a generation. This is her ring that I am sending to you.

Of course it may be that your relationship with the young lady you have told us about does not mature that far, in which case you should store the ring away for the future. It may also be that your young lady may have other ideas about what sort of engagement ring she would like to have – one that she chooses herself. That would be quite understandable, jewellery is such a personal thing, and it may not be to her taste. Also, she might feel it appropriate that *you* buy the ring that she wears as her engagement ring, in which case maybe she would like to wear it as a dress ring, like I did, or perhaps sell it and put the money towards a ring that you choose together. Of course in the future you may have a daughter of your own, and maybe would like to put this away for the next generation.

I have always said that gifts should be entirely unconditional; that you don't give somebody a present and tell them how to use, display or wear it. I shan't be insulted if I never see your young lady wearing it. I shan't be insulted if she hates it and sells it, that would be entirely her choice.

For the moment it is yours, and with it I give you my very best love for your future, whatever that may hold.

Much love

Mum

Hedge Fund

I love this little bit of the hedge that has remained uncut, it's a fabulous leaping off point. It sticks up a good thirty centimetres above the rest of the hedge, and there are another dozen or so just the same along the length of this mixed hedge in this suburban front garden. Mostly we sparrows are very territorial. We will live en masse in one garden, yet the next door plot attracts not a single one of us. This is because we value our privacy. The no go zones in between our territories help to preserve our safety too.

But that is to talk in generalities. Here I am being specific. This is a bungalow zone, lots of older people, so we try to put on a good display of something to entertain the old dears as they look out of their windows. In this, the centre of three houses that make up my territory, there is the hedge and a birdbath. The stone birdbath is quite near the window, but we know to always be cautious. We drink or bathe a few at a time, taking it in turns to stand guard and warn the others of danger. It works really well. One early evening I counted sixteen of us, either on the birdbath or waiting in turn on the hedge and nearby plants. There's a dead shrub in the corner of the garden. I thought the oldies were either not strong enough to pull it up and put it on the compost, or maybe they thought it was meant to look like that, but no. I overheard one of them talking about it.

'It's not really unsightly,' she was saying, 'hidden by the hedge like that, and I can't see it from the window as the curtain hides it. I leave it there because the little sparrows seem to use it a lot. They can see all around for predators before hopping over to the birdbath, so I like to think I'm doing them a bit of a favour.' Isn't that nice of her?

Next door to one side is a bird feeder. She was given it for Christmas, and passed it on to us, which is lovely. She keeps it well topped up, and hangs fat balls from it too, so there's plenty of food, especially as she has one of those bug hotels on the side of her wall, so we get a really varied diet, and fresh too. At the house on the other side there's a bird table, flat with a little roof to keep out the worst of the weather. The lady there puts a small bowl of water out too. So we get loads of variety, and it doesn't matter if one of them is away. There's still plenty to eat and drink.

Of course not all birds are the same. Some like to feed off a flat table, others like to perch, clinging on to a fat ball, or a wire cage with food in. I learned something the other day. I thought all of us birds drank like we do – slurp up a beakful of water then tip the head back to swallow; but no – wood pigeons are different. I watched one land on the birdbath. They come in like jumbo jets landing and the whole thing wobbles, but they drink with their heads down, like people do through a straw. I suppose because they're so big they don't have to be as watchful as we do, and generally they come down one at a time.

Other birds come down too of course. There are a couple of blackbirds that use the birdbath. They are very polite. They wait on the nearest branch if any of us are already using the facilities, and only come down when we've finished. Isn't that lovely? The neighbours, human and avian are one of the reasons we love it round here. There were five sparrow nests dotted along this hedge last year! Five! It was like Coronation Street I tell you, all the gossip and chattering between the various families, and sometimes you had to wait quite a few minutes to get on the feeders or on the birdbath.

The best bit about living here though, is this hedge by far. It marks the boundary between this small front garden, which isn't anything special, and the footpath and is made up of a mixed collection of shrubs. There is pyracantha as well as berberis and holly, all of which have tasty berries. There is also hawthorn and some roses, so we have a real mixture. They're called evergreen, because they keep their leaves on all year round. No matter how carefully the oldies look, the hedge is so thick that they never actually know how many nests we have in here. I'm not sure that evergreen is the right word really, some of the plants aren't green at all – winter or summer. The berberis for example, is a sort of dark purplish red. It all makes for a real variety of berries though, all these different plants close together. All of these plants also have prickles, spines or thorns, but have you ever watched a sparrow land on a slender branch? We know exactly how to land and not hurt ourselves. It always makes me very proud that we can do this, yet big birds, especially water birds like swans and geese are so clumsy coming into land, especially on a large expanse of water like a lake or a canal. I've seen them a couple of times and they make me laugh.

Some of these plants in the hedge grow more quickly than others, so the gardener employed by the householder has to keep doing a bit of pruning, but he has very strict instructions. From April to about the end of August, depending on the weather, we are very busy laying eggs, usually two and sometimes three clutches to give the best chances for our babies, or some of them, to survive.

Last year he gave the hedge its final trim of the year quite early. I was not happy. I'd been out collecting insects, spiders and worms for the family. This year our young are fully fledged now and ready to go and find their own way in the world, but on that occasion, I came back and you could have knocked me down with one of my own feathers! The gardener had taken a power hedge trimmer to the length of the whole hedge – scalped it. I landed on the bird bath and stood there with my beak open in amazement, I was so cross; I stood for ages with my wings on my hips, shouting that I had never asked for open-plan! It pretty quickly greened up again, but for a week or two you could see right through from one side of the hedge to the other in places. That was a bit scary, especially for the youngsters.

Now you may not know this, but it's against the law to *harm nesting birds or their eggs*. There's even an Act, especially to support us. It's called the Wildlife and Countryside Act of 1981. It's nice to know that someone cares about us. I would argue that any pruning of hedges potentially harms us, in that it can frighten us and/or our babies, and interfere with our privacy, perhaps making us more of a target for predators. There are so many cats living round here, you wouldn't believe it. So, guidance from the RSPB is that no pruning is done between the end of March and the beginning of autumn, depending on the weather. Sometimes we don't get started till quite late.

In theory we are protected by law, but that's the theory. We are very lucky in that the oldie we live near has given her gardener strict instructions that this hedge may not be cut until after August. Her gardener huffs and puffs, saying that the hedge looks a mess, and given his own way I suspect that he would get out that electric hedge trimmer again tomorrow.

But as it is, I've just seen him drive away in his white van, and we're safe for at least another week. I've got to go now, I saw one of the oldies clean out the birdbath and top it up a few minutes ago. I'm next on the rota to stand guard while some of the youngest sparrows drink and bathe, then it will be my turn.

Opposites Attract

Gayle was as quiet as she could be with the key in the lock, and then closing the door once she was inside, but it was no good. All around her tiny pairs of eyes shot open from where her books had been snoozing on the shelves, and peered closely at the bag she was carrying. It could have been anything in there, groceries, cosmetics, alcohol, although she had to admit that, whether she had been just to the supermarket, or into town, as often as not it contained new or borrowed books.

Today she had two ordinary supermarket carrier bags, but the shape was enough to give the game away. Those things in one of her shopping bags were definitely books. The books on the shelf muttered to each other.

She always carried with her a plastic Waterstones bag. Her own new books, library books, and the books she sometimes borrowed from friends at book club mustn't get wet. It didn't matter how hard she tried to fool them, the existing books always seemed to know.

The books on the hall shelves rolled their eyes and continued to grumble quietly amongst themselves. More books! More competition for space, and even less chance that they would be read next. The sighs and grumbles in the hallway were audible, even some tutting from the second shelf, where the residents could best see the shopping bags, and guess the number of books inside.

'She's bought more books.' The word quickly spread through the shelves that lined the hallway and, as if by osmosis, through the door into the living room. Even from the bedroom there came a very faint, but definite, rumble of discontent.

Gayle sighed too. One day she would get away with it. One day she would sneak into the flat and nobody, or rather no books, would notice. It was ridiculous to feel guilty about spending her own money, and because of the censorious attitude of pieces of paper. One day! But that day wasn't today.

With a sigh she emptied the bag onto the table, four new books. One was a beautifully bound copy of a book by Virginia Woolf, picked up in that smart second-hand book shop in town; then there was the biography of Agatha Christie that she had fancied reading for a while that she had picked up in Waterstones. Then there was a pure impulse buy; two paperback novels ideal for bedtime reading. She had found these during the routine grocery shop when, passing down the aisle of magazines and publications, she had spotted these latest two in a series of paperbacks that she had really enjoyed. They were a good price too, and without a second thought she had popped a copy of each into her trolley.

Ignoring her existing stock of books, who were getting more and more unsettled now, these latter two she took through to the bedroom and put them on the bedside table, pushing out of the way a precariously-balanced pile of seven or so, all waiting their turn. The hardbacks she squeezed into the living room bookcase, moving a couple of historical novels into the hall to make room. The grumbles were getting louder now.

'What you fail to understand,' Gayle muttered to these bad-tempered little friends of hers, 'is that there are two distinctly different hobbies involved here: collecting books and reading books. If I never bought another book in my life, I reckon that I would have to live to be two hundred and fifty years old at least, to read all the ones I already have.'

Gayle never ceased to marvel at something her father had pointed out to her years before; that every book she ever read in English or any other Germanic language, was made up of just the same twenty-six letters. All the emotion and information she ever took on board, was a combination of those twenty-six squiggles, just in a different order. At the time, and ever afterwards when she thought about it, it was mind-blowing. Now though, was not the time for such deep thinking. For tonight Gayle had a date with a young man.

*

This would be their third outing and she was

really looking forward to it. The first had been a leisurely cup of coffee after they met in the local library. Both had reached for the same book, laughed about it in an *After you, No after you,* sort of way, then got talking. Rob seemed very nice, and had the added advantage that he too was very keen on books and reading. They laughed together that it was a significant place for them to meet. Kindred spirits, Gayle decided.

On that first, and then on their second date they had talked about their favourite authors, preferred genre of story, and found that they both preferred the reality of an old-fashioned book. They had agreed that electronic books had their uses, such as when they were going on holiday, but there was nothing like the feel and smell, especially of a new printed book. This would be their third date, and tonight, for the first time, she had invited Rob into her flat at the end of the evening, rather than a quick kiss before she waved him off in his car.

She opened the door and led him in. He stood for a moment, taking in his surroundings.

'This is lovely, Gayle. I love the decoration and those bookshelves are fabulous. What a great idea.' She felt pleased. She had a number of bookcases throughout the living room and bedroom, but had quickly run out of space. Needing something fairly inexpensive she had resorted to four planks of wood stretched across piles of breeze blocks, along one wall in the hall. The arrangement had been much admired by her friends, and clearly Rob liked it too. She left him looking through the books while she made a pot of coffee. And then he blew it – big time.

As she returned to the living room with the tray, Rob was extracting a beautifully illustrated copy of Wuthering Heights that had been given to her for her birthday. He turned to the frontispiece and read the inscription, bending the pages right back in the process, until the spine cracked. Gayle was horrified. Who but an animal would treat a beautiful book like that? Especially as it was someone else's book?

'Sometimes,' he said, 'these hefty books just won't lie flat will they?' and he did it again.

'Now where's that section? Oh yes, here we are,' he gave the spine another tug, 'I'll mark it for you, then you can read it later and see if you agree.'

'I'll get you a bookmark,' she croaked, rummaging for something suitable on the table.

'Oh, don't worry. This'll do it.' Then he committed the crime to exceed all crimes according to Gayle. He turned over the corner of a page of one of her books.

She hadn't realised what a strange noise she must have made: something between a groan and a wail.

'What's the matter?' he asked, genuinely confused, 'You're surely not one of those people who think that books should be handled like porcelain? Oh dear. My bookshelves are groaning with books that have been *really* enjoyed, and it shows. Some of the spines are so creased that they can hardly be read. There are loose pages in some where they have come unglued. You can't lie in bed, or eat your breakfast one-handed without bending the spines back, can you?' He was getting into his stride now, 'A book is a tool Gayle, a workhorse. If you love a book so much that it gets battered, that's a sign of how much you've cared. Go to a bookshop or on line and buy another copy. Better still, if you care so much about, say, a signed copy of a book like this one, then don't read it. Put it on the bookshelf and just worship its pristine condition. Anything else doesn't make sense.'

Gayle took the book off him, and straightened out the dog-eared corner. Then, as she kept a tight hold of it, she picked up on his first point, 'You read while you're having breakfast?' she whispered, not really wanting to know the answer.

'Oh, yes! I don't get a lot of free time, so it would be a shame not to use it. I'm quite the multi-tasker.' He grinned at her as if he had said something clever. 'Of course I have a tissue handy, in case I spill anything. It wouldn't do to have pages permanently stuck together.'

Gayle felt a bit weak, 'And you read in bed?' She read in bed too, but sitting up so she could hold the book carefully.

He laughed, pulling another volume out of her shelves, while she sat watching, transfixed with horror.

'All the time. Many's the night I've nodded off and woken in the early hours, with the book rucked up in the bedding, or I'm lying on top of it, or it's fallen on the floor. I've lost count of the times I've had to sellotape loose pages back in.'

He casually threw the book down onto the sofa, from where it slid onto the floor landing open and face down, with three pages bent in half.

'And there's this one, I enjoyed this one,' he was saying, yanking another hefty volume out of the shelves. They had been tightly packed and two other books moved forward threateningly.

Rob flicked through the pages, 'You don't make notes?' he asked. 'How do you remind yourself of the particular passages you want to go back to? You don't turn down pages, and you don't make margin notes.'

He seemed genuinely interested. Gayle picked up the fallen book and laid it carefully on her knee.

'I always have a notebook handy. I write down anything I want to go back to in that. You write margin notes in your books? You actually write in them?'

'Well, yes of course I do. You use a notebook? What a faff. Much more sensible to write on the book itself, in the margin, then turn down the corner so you can find it easily. Usually only in pencil, but you can't always just put your hands on a pencil can you, so sometimes in biro. I usually have a biro in my pocket.'

Gayle's eyes widened in horror, 'I'm sorry Rob, I'm going to have to ask you to go now. I'm not feeling at all well.'

She saw him out, and flopped on the sofa, nursing the two books that had been violated, and gently smoothing their pages.

Later that night, when Gayle had gone to bed, the books on the shelves whispered quietly to themselves.

'Much better,' they agreed, 'to be loved and cherished and wait our turn, however long it takes, to be read by someone like Gayle, than to be mutilated and abused by someone like him.'

'Notes in the margin, sometimes in Biro,' said the Agatha Christie biography, 'and turning pages over at the corner, that must be painful.'

'It is,' confirmed the copy of Wuthering Heights, 'and those creases never come out properly.'

'We're much better off here with Gayle, you know,' one of the older books offered, 'she really cares for us and looks after us. We're held gently and dusted every week. And there's really plenty of room for us all, even when she does bring in newcomers.'

'*Two distinctly different hobbies* – that's what she said earlier. We aren't just any old books to be misused and then discarded or replaced, we are collectors' pieces to be treasured.'

As if of one accord, the books straightened up their spines and shuffled along the shelves to helpfully make more room for more of Gayle's new purchases.

For she would surely be going shopping again tomorrow.

Uncle Maurice's Car

As car accidents went it wasn't at all serious. Two cars containing members of the same extended family, destined for the same holiday cottage, in the days long before seatbelts. My family and I were in the second car and we had covered some hundred and fifty miles quite happily in tandem without incident.

Then, approaching Bristol, we reached a main road at a T-junction, where we needed to turn left. The front car, my Uncle Maurice's, seemed to pull forward as if to make the manoeuvre, then he hesitated and stopped, presumably because of a fast-moving car coming along the main road from the right.

My dad, driving our car immediately behind him, glanced to the right to check the oncoming traffic just as Uncle Maurice hit the brakes, and our car slid gently into the back of his. The speed was so low and the touch so slight, that Uncle Maurice merely lowered his driver's window and pretend-shook his fist at my dad, laughing all the time, much to the amazement of two women standing on the footpath beside us. If they had been hoping for a set-to between the men, they were to be disappointed, although they must have been perplexed at the laughter that broke out in both cars.

When we reached our destination, an inspection showed minor damage to both bumpers, their rear and our front. At this time cars did not have integral bumpers, but chrome affairs that were bolted to each end of the car.

It was fortuitous that my sister was dating a car mechanic when this happened, and when we got home Daz offered immediately to get both the cars sorted out. It would be quite a straightforward job and he would only need to borrow Uncle Maurice's car overnight to take it to the workshop at his friend's house.

The following weekend, my dad drove Daz, my sister, and I to Uncle Maurice's house. Dad drove our car back home, and Daz and my sister said I could go along with them in Uncle Maurice's car to his friend Tony's.

Tony was a motor mechanic who lived near the canal and adjacent to a popular pub. The access to his workshop was down a series of narrow lanes. Driving along one of these lanes, the road suddenly bends sharply to the left, and at that point an even-more-narrow lane goes off to the right. We pulled up behind a car that was waiting, indicating to turn right, presumably on his way down to the pub.

A car approached from the opposite direction, driving too fast to take the sharp bend safely. To avoid a head-on collision, the driver in the car in front of us slammed his car in reverse, and drove backwards, albeit quite slowly, into Uncle Maurice's front bumper.

So, now we had damage to both the front and the back of my uncle's car, much to Tony's surprise when we arrived at his workshop.

Over the course of the evening the car was repaired and Uncle Maurice was delighted with the job they had made of the back. Of course, he had no idea that there had been any damage to the front.

At that time it was not a requirement to declare whether a car had been involved in an accident when it was put up for sale, and it was only many years later, long after he had sold the car that we told Uncle Maurice the whole story.

Diamonds are Forever

It had long been a weekend ritual. On Saturday nights Mark and his parents went to the golf club, he and his father played nine holes of golf in the afternoon, then his mother joined them for a meal.

Everything changed when Mark's father died and the golf club visits lost their appeal. His mother however, was an attractive woman, still only in her forties, and she was soon to be seen out and about with a single man of her own age. Within a few months Arthur became a fixture in his mother's life, and the Saturday evening get-togethers were reinstated, but with a difference.

Arthur was a lovely gentle man, hailing from Liverpool, some forty miles away. He declared himself not to be of their class, explaining that he was brought up in a council house, in a rough area of the city. Nevertheless Mark liked the way Arthur treated his mother, and the two men, so very different in background, got on very well.

The difference in the weekend routine was that on Saturday evenings they would visit not the golf club, but The Working Men's Club in the area of Liverpool where Arthur was well-known. This was a very different sort of evening, with a cabaret and a bingo session, which was taken very seriously. On his first visit Mark started speaking to Arthur during the bingo, and was soundly shushed by people at all the surrounding tables. They took their bingo very seriously.

One week when they were due at the Working Men's Club Arthur announced that he had a different idea. There was a programme of entertainment coming to a pub not far away. It was very highly thought of, and not dissimilar to the Club they usually went to. Arthur was keen to take them. They arranged that Mark would drive his mother to Liverpool and meet Arthur at the pub. He was told that once he left the motorway, there were only two right turns and the pub was directly ahead. He was to leave the motorway at the first exit after PAUL.

This meant nothing, but he told Mark that he would easily spot PAUL on the right-hand side of the motorway when he got to the right place, as indeed he did. Local Scallies, as Arthur called them, had stolen roof slates from one of the pairs of council houses – these days known as social housing – that was clearly visible from the motorway. The missing tiles made a pattern that spelled out PAUL. Immediately he reached it, Mark pulled over to the left and found the pub with no difficulty.

They settled at their table, with chicken in a

basket ordered from the bar. His mother had a sherry, and Mark and Arthur each had a couple of bottles of Double Diamond.

The entertainment was a great success, not unlike that in the Working Men's Club, but perhaps a step up the social scale. There was a magician – of the sort whose act goes deliberately wrong for laughs, a couple of comedians, the ubiquitous bingo session and a pop group, but the best was saved for the last. Arthur had not told them about the act that was to top the bill. She was a singer, tall, well-built with impeccable hair and make-up, and sinuous was the word that came to Mark's mind.

She wore a floor-length pale blue dress in a silver embroidered fabric. Teamed with that she had on elbow-length white gloves, with a number of bangles on each wrist. She also had heavily ornate earrings and a heavy-looking sparkly necklace. Mark vaguely wondered whether they had come here because Arthur was trying his hand at matchmaking, but Arthur's face was inscrutable. Mark thought that this statuesque young woman was a real beauty. Her voice matched her appearance, and she sang half a dozen songs, *Big Spender*, *Downtown*, *Big Yellow Taxi*, *Diamonds are Forever*, and a couple of others. She was particularly suited, both vocally and visually to the Shirley Bassey songs.

What stood out for Mark particularly, was her last number – the ever popular hit from Dusty Springfield, *You Don't Have to Say you Love Me*. By this time, everyone in the pub was singing along. At the finale of this number, the singer, whose name Mark soon forgot such was his shock, removed her wig with one hand, whereon her voice dropped by a whole octave, and to the great shock of Mark and many in the audience, she was clearly revealed to be a man in drag.

Fava Beans and a Nice Chianti

As commutes go, Lloyd's had to be one of the better ones, a short bus ride down the hill, then a half mile walk along the unmade track over the railway line. The track had little traffic, serving just one large detached house standing in its own grounds, with its neatly manicured garden and a substantial pond. The track then crossed the railway track into a farmyard, and was by that point, just a public footpath. Vehicles visiting the farm approached it from the far side, where Lloyd's office was on the main road.

It was nearly the end of March. At about this time last year, on taking this regular walk, Lloyd had come across several corpses of what he had assumed were frogs. He was unclear on the difference between species of amphibian, even more so when they had been squashed, as some of these evidently had. In his mind's eye Lloyd imagined small boys playing and tormenting the amphibians over the weekend, as they might in a book in Enid Blyton's time. He regularly met an older man who passed him on the track after collecting his morning paper, and Lloyd mentioned the carnage to him. The older man had an explanation. The frogs felt an imperative urge to reach the water to spawn, and while they were out in the open, they are vulnerable to getting run over by vehicles. Lloyd had no alternative suggestion, but it seemed unlikely. There was so little traffic from this single house and, whilst some of the little corpses looked rather flat and deflated a couple, on the contrary, seemed quite bloated.

He saw no more on subsequent days, and had forgotten all about it. Then this year he came across many more of the corpses; several dozen at least he counted. It seemed impossible that so many could be hit by vehicles over the period of one night; especially as, once again, several of them were bloated rather than flattened. As Lloyd peered more closely he could see that many of these dead creatures had blood oozing from their sides. The blood was bright red as it might be from a human, and he was a little bit surprised that cold-blooded amphibians would be so colourful.

He decided that the old guy who had given him an explanation last year, must be wrong, and determined as soon as he got home from work to search the internet for the real reason. It didn't take long. He keyed in *Exploding Frogs* as that seemed to best describe what he had seen. There was nothing, but there was plenty under *Exploding Toads,* and it wasn't very pleasant.

The old guy had been partly right. These were

toads, which lived most of the year in the undergrowth below the trees on one side of the track. They caught and ate insects, and needed the shade to stay cool.

Where he had also been correct was that they had the compelling urge to find water in which to spawn, and having found it, the memory of where the water was situated would be handed down generation to generation. Over the years many, many toads would take the risk of coming out into the open to cross the track to reach the water, and then go back. Even when they intuited that it was unsafe, they felt compelled to make the journey.

The true reason was clearly explained on the internet. Over a period of time crows, of which many inhabited this woodland, had come to learn that they very much liked the taste of toads' liver. They had perfected the art of swooping down when the toads were out in the open and vulnerable, pecking a small hole in the side of the amphibian, and ripping out its tasty liver, all in one smooth action.

The natural defence technique for toads under attack is to inflate themselves by taking in air, in order to look big and ferocious in the hope of fending off an attacker. This is what these toads had done, but they each had the hole in their side, and had lost their liver. The action of inflating themselves merely pushed their innards out through the hole, making them look as if they had exploded. In some cases, they may subsequently have been run over, but it was more likely that the whole of their innards had been propelled out through the wound in their side at considerable pressure, leaving them looking like an empty husk. Others, generally the larger ones, had only got as far as inflating themselves when they died of loss of blood, and of course, their livers had been ripped out. Lloyd turned off the computer and went downstairs, where his mother was serving up their evening meal.

'I thought we'd have liver and onions tonight, Lloyd. I know you like it, and we haven't had it for a while.'

Lloyd looked at the plate of raw offal, 'Maybe not tonight, Mum, sorry. I do like it, but I think I'll just get myself something else tonight.'

Roses Grow on You

Miriam went as often as she could to visit her Uncle Reg. He had lived in Arbour Court Residential Home for several years, since he could no longer manage on his own. As usual Miriam made small talk with Chantelle, the specific carer allocated to her uncle. He was, she said, fiercely independent but becoming ever more frail. Through her infrequent visits Miriam could see his deterioration for herself. They would sit and chat for a while, would take Mungo her dog to see the various residents parked in the communal lounge and then Miriam would take Uncle Reg for lunch at the local pub, where dogs were welcome.

Miriam had been determined to visit Reg this week. It was early November and, where she lived in the Scottish hills, it may be that she would be snowed in within weeks and not able to visit him until the spring.

It took some manoeuvring and seemed to take longer each time to get Reg into the car at Arbour Court and out again at the pub, then do the same in reverse after lunch. When Miriam returned him to the care home they sat chatting for a while in his room. After a cup of coffee, as she made a move to set off for home he asked her to stay where she was a little longer, as he had something for her.

He spent some time struggling to retrieve something from the floor of his wardrobe, but after much huffing and puffing he produced a beautiful bouquet of perfect white roses.

He offered them to Miriam with a big grin, 'I remembered, you see?'

Miriam was puzzled. Remembered what exactly, she wondered.

'They are lovely Uncle Reg. Thank you.' But her confusion must have shown on her face.

'What?' he said, 'I'm right aren't I? Don't say I got it wrong.'

'Er, I'm not sure,' Miriam was at a loss what to say. This was awkward.

'Your wedding anniversary of course,' Reg said, and waited for her response.

'It's really lovely of you, but I think you must have confused us with another couple. Our wedding anniversary is in the spring, March in fact.'

''I haven't got it wrong. It's in the book I'm sure.' He made his way to a chest of drawers from which he produced a small hard backed book. 'This was your aunty's address book,' his fumbling hands searched the pages, until he found what he was looking for.

'Here it is – *Miriam's wedding 4th November 1998.* See? Tomorrow is your twenty fifth wedding anniversary.' He sounded triumphant.

'Oh, Uncle Reg, you darling.' Miriam put her arms around him. 'You're quite right, I did get married on 4th November 1998, but that was to my first husband. Remember? We got divorced five years later. Steve and I have been married six years next March.'

'Oh no, I see what I've done,' he looked stricken then started to laugh. 'What a fool I am.'

'It's the thought that counts Uncle Reg, and this was a lovely thought.'

'Just one thing,' he said as she prepared to leave, 'I asked Chantelle to go out especially and get me the flowers, and I told her why. Can we just keep this between ourselves? Otherwise she'll think I've gone daft.'

As Miriam left through the front hall, Chantelle was at Reception.

'I believe you played a part in getting these for me, Chantelle. They are beautiful. Thank you so much.'

Over Chantelle's shoulder, Miriam saw Uncle Reg wink at her.

What Goes Around, Comice Around

Ellie Bruce took the parcel into the kitchen and scored through the securing parcel tape. It was good that this had arrived on her day off work. Plants arriving by post can't be left too long before being put outside, and don't benefit from being left on the doorstep in the sun. The weather today was perfect for planting. She was surprised at the size of the box, the plants must be more mature than she had expected.

Everything was ready, a bucket of water to soak the roots, the spade to dig suitable holes. She had already decided where to put the new fruit trees and was looking forward to reaping the harvest of apples and of plums.

On opening the big parcel there seemed to be more than the four bare-rooted stems that she had ordered and paid for, two plums and two apples. She counted them out on to the counter gently untangling the roots. Yes, there were six dual-fruited trees in the parcel. The idea of the dual-fruited tree was that two juvenile trees were grafted onto the same dwarf rootstock. This meant that theoretically, the two different varieties would pollinate each other. She checked them again. There were the two dwarf apples, each containing a Bramley and a Braeburn cultivar. The next two were the plums she had ordered, grafted in the same way, a Victoria and a variety Ellie was unfamiliar with – Reine claude d'althan.

She turned her attention to the two remaining trees - the mystery trees. These were pears. Pears that she hadn't ordered, but again they were dual trees combining Conference and Comice varieties. Checking the invoice that she hadn't been overcharged, or ordered incorrectly, she understood what had happened. The small print pointed out that orders over a certain value would receive additional trees as a gift.

Nobody in the family was that keen on pears. Ellie was happy to eat one now and then, but they seemed one of those fruits that stubbornly remained rock hard with a period of about five minutes when they were perfect, before they were over-ripe and turned to mush. Still, the trees would bring insects into the garden and that could only be good.

The crop that first year was phenomenal; the trees were so weighted down with fruit that the branches were almost trailing on the ground; especially the pears. One tree had a total of twenty one, and the other, slightly larger and more robust tree, had forty eight separate fruits. She read up a little about the pears and discovered that they could both be picked at the same time, then ripening would continue in a warm kitchen, with the Comice pears taking a couple of extra weeks ripening time beyond the Conference. She read that Conference were the usual type of pear you might buy in the supermarket. Comice pears, the big fat ones she learned could be eaters, but were also excellent for cooking. In the same way as one might stew apples, Ellie supposed. There was no way that the family would use all these. Ellie selected what they could use, then took the rest to the monthly book club meeting along with a roll of plastic bags. Every single pear found a new home so at least they weren't wasted.

A month or two later there was a Book Sale at the church and amongst the cakes on sale were slices of a pear-flavoured tray bake! No baker herself, she took a few home to share with the family and they were delicious. It was only later that she learned that some of her friends had kept the Conference pears for their own use, and handed over the Comice pears to the team of baking ladies. Some of Ellie's pears had ended up back where they started.

The blossom on Ellie's fruit trees, especially the two pear trees, was very sparse this year. She had only seen a couple of bunches of blossom and these were quickly battered to the ground by rain and strong winds in May. She doubted that there would be such a good harvest. She weeded the beds, pruned and fed the trees and let them rest.

Hopefully next year they'll be back up to full production again.

Because, as the old saying goes: *What goes around, comes around*; or in the case of Ellie's pear trees, What goes around *Comice* around.

The Blue Shoes

They had been invited to a wedding. Joanne had her outfit all sorted, a silver-blue trouser suit, under which she would wear a blouse in shades of turquoise, blue and silver. All she needed now was the shoes. And there was the problem. She had not worn shoes with high heels for years, they played havoc with her aches and pains and so she allowed herself plenty of time to go shoe-shopping. She fancied blue, to tone in with the blouse. She packed the blouse safely in a bag and went into town.

She had thought about buying on line, in fact had sent for two pairs a couple of months in advance, but there was a problem. Midway between a size three and a size four, and with one foot definitely larger than the other, nothing ever seemed to fit. She tried on both pairs then made the trek to the post office to send them both back.

For some unknown reason the skin on

Joanne's feet had always been tender. She used to look on in amazement as her mother would try on shoes, say 'Yes, these are fine,' and that was the end of the transaction. She had even seen her mother keep new shoes on, and wear them home from the shop. This was what her mother called *wearing them in*. Joanne herself knew that new shoes would need *wearing in*. In her own case though, it always seemed touch and go whether or not new shoes would be *worn in* before they were in fact *worn out*.

Four shops were tried without success, then at last she thought of Marks and Spencer. She had thought that suede may be soft and so more comfortable; there was sometimes a lot of standing around a wedding. Marks and Spencer had one suitable pair; not suede, a slightly more casual canvas type of fabric, but the colour was perfect and the heel was flat. She took a couple of turns around the small carpeted area and checked out the mirror. 'Those look nice,' said another woman customer, 'Are they comfy?' Joanne smiled. It was too complicated to explain and time was getting on.

Trying on the shoes again at home they still looked just as good, but felt a little more unforgiving than they had in the shop. Joanne had formulated a plan. She would wear the shoes for an increasing length of time each afternoon, just around the house, and maybe on the driveway to make sure the soles weren't too slippery. As she eased them off again that first time, she added *Box of Sticking Plasters* to her shopping list on the front of the fridge. For indeed wearing them around the house was not only about softening them up, it was also about deciding where protective sticking plasters would need to be applied to minimise the discomfort and the damage on the day.

After two days, each with twenty minutes in the shoes, Joanne found herself walking rather like a cowboy just dismounted from his horse. There were several red marks apparent on the tops of both feet and on her toes, and the beginnings of a blister on her heel. She changed the shopping list to read *2 Boxes of Sticking Plasters*, determined not to give in.

For eight solid days Joanne persevered. Eight solid days of what rapidly became discomfort and misery, and there were only five more until the wedding. Doggedly she had gone about the routines of day to day living. Having anticipated that by now she would be able to wear the shoes all day, this was a big disappointment. And it was that ninth afternoon that she first noticed a definite squeak as she walked about the house. Each time she took a step with the left shoe it squeaked. She tried outside, walking to the gate and back to the front door, there was a definite, quite discernible squeak. So not only was she now in considerable discomfort, but everyone would hear her moving around. Joanne gave up ... what on earth was she going to do?

In desperation she went to the spare bedroom and pulled out all the old shoe boxes, some of which had been in there for years, and there she found them. Completely forgotten and not worn for at least eight years she found a pair of leather open-toed sandals. When she used to routinely holiday abroad, she would take them to slip on and off around the pool, and yes, they were comfortable. Gingerly she tried them on.

They were still comfortable, the straps around the back of the foot were made of elastic and forgiving. They weren't quite flat, but flat enough and infinitely more comfortable than the blue shoes. They were of a metallic pewter coloured finish, still smart enough to be seen, and they neither rubbed her feet nor did they squeak. Perfect.

The wedding was beautiful, and Joanne was comfortable for the whole day. She put a rubber band around the blue shoes to keep them together, and a note inside "Brand new, unworn", then she put them in the sack the next time the charity collectors came. They were beautiful shoes, and somebody would no doubt love them and find them comfortable, but not Joanne. As life got back to normal for her, she crossed *Sticking Plasters* off the shopping list.

Freddie Flies the Nest

Well, not exactly flies the nest because of course he couldn't actually fly, but he hoped today to be able to leave home. It was Freddie's final examination this afternoon. He had just one more task to achieve in order to demonstrate that he was ready to go out into the world on his own. He glanced nervously across at his mother, who smiled encouragingly. Then he concentrated hard and he . . . jumped. Fantastic! The jump was measured at fifty times his body length, and reaching nearly two feet in height. That's sixty times his body height, pretty impressive for a young flea, and Freddie had only hatched from his cocoon early that very morning. It was only a matter of a few weeks since he had been a tiny white egg.

His mother beamed at his success, but it was with mixed emotions. Freddie's success meant that it was time for him to move out of the family home, find himself a partner and set up his own family on a new host. The host who accommodated them currently could not handle another family added to those already in residence. They would be spotted, especially if the host was noticed to be scratching more than usual. Then they would meet the fate dreaded by all fleas – being bathed and then doused with flea powder.

If no alternative host was available, then Freddie's life, sadly, was likely to be short unless he could find a suitable carpet or similar in which to wait. He was capable, like most fleas, of waiting up to a couple of years, but the conditions really needed to be perfect for that to be possible. It would be better by far to move today, or tomorrow at the latest, onto a fluffy dog, where he could snuggle down and raise his own family.

Later, as they walked in the park on their family host, his mother offered him some advice.

'Go for a dog with a medium length coat, Freddie,' she told him. 'If you go for a dog with very short hair, you are too easy for humans to spot. Very long hair on a dog can be good for hiding – think of the comparison between living in a forest or woodland, and open grassland. It's great to be under all that growth, but the downside is that those owners will know that too, and they will be very vigilant.

'Don't choose a hound,' she told him, watching Freddie eyeing up a handsome beagle. 'I know they have ear flaps that can provide dark places to hide, and dark places, now you are grown-up, are easier to hide in than light. For some reason though beagles and a few other breeds seem to give off less carbon dioxide than others, and that is something we need plenty of. Nor do they spend a lot of time licking their skin and their paws, and they don't pant much. Your cousin tried one once. One bite he took, that's all and he had to spit it out, it tasted so foul. Then he had to immediately relocate to a little terrier. Unless there is a health problem with a hound, they are really not the best from a flea's point of view.'

His mother was a wise flea. She had overheard the owner of their host talking to a beagle owner. This person had said that the kennels from which her dog had been acquired, and which had a number of Crufts' successes to its name, never treated their beagles for fleas. "They just never seem to need it. We keep a watchful eye of course, but Barney is our third beagle and, touch wood, we've never seen a flea."'

'What do I go for then, Ma?' Freddie needed as much information as possible, and his mother gave it some thought.

'These fashionable curly-coated dogs, Cockerpoos and such, are a bit of an unknown quantity as hosts as yet. Personally I would go for a darkish coloured, medium haired dog. Spaniels tend to be a good bet, and we've always been quite happy here on our Schnauzer. Maybe a border collie or a retriever or a setter,' she mused. 'Mongrels are good too, they are quite rufty-tufty and don't make a fuss. I think they're maybe less likely to scratch a lot and so draw attention to you and your family.'

'My family,' Freddie smiled at her, 'I'm going to have my own family, Ma.'

'Tell you what,' she said to him, 'When we're out for our walk on the schnauzer tomorrow morning

I'll point out some likely passers-by, but you'll have to trust me and be ready to jump.'

Next morning the dog, his owner and the flea family went for their morning walk as usual. They skirted round the children's playground and across the road into the park. There a man was approaching them, with two spaniels on leads. They brushed up close to the schnauzer, and Freddie's mother whispered to him, 'This is it son. These two look ideal. I've packed you a few eggs to start you off. Keep them warm and in no time you'll have your own little family breeding.

But – make sure that you're not seen. Put the eggs behind the ears on the darker of the two dogs. If you're lucky they may already have a few residents and you can just increase the colony.'

As the darker of the two dogs came close to the schnauzer, and while the two humans talked about the weather and other boring stuff, Freddie grabbed his chance. He jumped higher than he had ever done before, and landed just behind the spaniel's ear as they each continued on their separate ways.

Freddie thrived. He found that another flea had recently moved onto the female spaniel, and when they got back to where the spaniels lived, there was a cosy little colony setting up already in the fluffy dog bed. That night the two dogs snuggled down together after a bit of a scratch and a lot of circling to get comfortable, and although it was only a few weeks before one of the fleas was spotted and dogs, bed and carpets were treated with flea powder, Freddie and one of the female fleas had managed to hide down the skirting board, ready to emerge once the effects of the powder had worn off. Then the two of them were able to begin the cycle all over again.

Techno Numpty

At my great age there are few things that really scare me, but one that absolutely terrifies me is the concept of driverless cars. So much goes wrong on a regular basis, in my opinion, with technology of all sorts, that I really hope that I am gone before they become the norm.

There are a number of reasons for my dislike of technology in general. I do use technology of course. I have a mobile phone, and a laptop. Somebody once asked whether I had an Android phone or a Smart phone; I didn't know, I guessed you might call it a Smartphone – because it's certainly smarter than I am. This phone is used for simple activities only; I make and receive calls, and I send and receive texts. I have learned how to take photographs too, which I can then upload to my laptop. Occasionally I post these onto social media to share with others. By social media I mean of course

Facebook. I ignore all other social media. I've never used TikTok, neither do I go on Instagram, YouTube or Reddit, or any of those sites.

I don't trust what used to be called Twitter. Logic dictated long ago that a post on Twitter was a Tweet. Nowadays, since the individual I have dubbed *Brain of America* bought the company and changed the name to X, nobody seems quite sure what to call the posts, so most people continue to call them Tweets. Most people indeed seem to continue to call X Twitter. One wonders what was the point of changing it at all.

The individual responsible is someone in whose knowledge and common sense I have very little faith. I think you'll agree if you watched, as I did, his attempt to launch a rocket. The rocket blew up almost immediately after take-off and he tried to posit that this was in fact a success as the rocket had left the ground, and he called the explosion a 'Rapid, unscheduled disassembly.' Yeah, right. If it was unscheduled and it rapidly disassembled into a myriad of small pieces immediately after take-off, then in my opinion it blew up.

Another cause for concern about the same individual is around his pioneering electric vehicles. Again, it seemed, he set himself up to fail although surely that stunt could not just have been to get people talking? It seems a very strange tactic if it was planned to fail.

What happened, in case you didn't see it, was that he invited somebody to try and break the glass on one of his vehicles, a Cybertruck with supposedly bulletproof windows. That's right, this man wasn't going to shoot at it, simply to throw a metal ball at the glass, with photographers poised to send the resulting photographs out into the ether. The hypothesis was, one presumes, that the glass would remain intact, and did it? No, it did not. The ball smashed into the driver's window, which shattered.

Unfazed he suggested that the person who was the thrower had thrown 'a little too hard,' and invited him to try again, this time with the back window. The throw was pretty puny, I could probably have achieved it, and the result was exactly the same. The vehicle now had two shattered windows. This is a guy throwing a metal ball at, supposedly, bullet proof glass! Not to be downhearted, our hero claimed to be delighted that the ball hadn't gone through the window, merely shattered it. Oh, so that's okay then. And I'm sure that any would-be shooter would be more than happy, in a real-life situation to be asked not to shoot it 'too hard.'

It sounds as though I am being negative about one individual, but in the interest of balance there are, as I said, lots of these sharing sites and I don't bother with any of the others either. The number of times domestic computers and apps crash is concerning. We all have come across the highly technical advice: 'Have you tried turning it off and turning it on again?' It doesn't fill me with confidence.

But I digress. I doubt whether rockets or bulletproof glass are going to feature heavily in what is left of my lifetime, unlike electric vehicles in general. Just a few weeks ago, I was out with my dog, walking along a minor tarmac road with no footpaths.

It was only when we turned off onto a cinder track, that I could hear the approach of a vehicle's tyres across the damp cinders. Moving into the side to let him pass, I caught up with him a few minutes later. Having delivered his parcel he was returning to his van. I apologised for delaying him, explaining that I had no idea he was behind me. We had quite a chat. He was clearly very unhappy with these vehicles, believing that it was only a matter of time before a pedestrian was killed.

*

The algorithms on social media I find amusing. As a crime writer I sometimes have occasion to explore, shall we say, unusual and diverse topics. So, having written a book involving a shooting I kept seeing ads for gun clubs on my facebook feed; then having explored the army's role in Northern Ireland in 1972 for another story, I received a mass of recruitment ads for the Army, (little do they know that I am seventy two with arthritis and a dicky hip!) They kept this campaign up for two years! All of these algorithms seem very persistent. I bought a bed-jacket on line as a gift nearly eight years ago, and the company I bought from have regularly bombard me with their ads ever since, even though I have never bought from them again.

I suspect that I may on several occasions, have offended people who are my Facebook friends, and who have asked me to share their posts on social media. Now, if I have three options – Like, Comment and Share, even I can figure out which one to wave my cursor at to share the post. But apparently there is another option whereby you don't use the share option, you are asked to 'Copy and Paste.' At this point I scroll on past. Several people have tried to explain it to me, 'You just tap your finger on the screen, hold, drag' or some such. Believe me, if I tap and hold my finger on the screen all I get is finger marks on the screen. Do I care? No, not really. But if I have done this to you, now at least you know why.

    I have resisted putting GPS on my phone. I prefer to check google maps before leaving home, maybe scribbling a little map or directions for in the car. It has led to some interesting detours to avoid accidents and road works over the years, but I used to travel all over England and Wales with my job. It served me well then, and has continued to do so since.

    Other aspects of technology I find equally baffling. I have no desire for a smart speaker to be turning on and off my lights and fire, nor calling down other family members from upstairs, I don't have an upstairs. No doubt they are a lot smarter than I am, but I'm fine without one, thank you. I am routinely asked whether or not I wish to continue with or without cookies. I always thought *cookies* were what Americans called biscuits! I was once offered a choice of two alternatives when I asked somebody for a copy of their promotional material, 'With the QR code, or without? I have both.'

    My response? 'Definitely without please.' I didn't own up that wouldn't know what to do with a QR code, eat it perhaps?

    I don't have to be flooded with spam, and bots

and trolls. Also I very seldom speak emoji, don't do podcasts, nor do I often share Gifs and memes, whatever they are. If it doesn't happen through just pressing the Share key then in my life it doesn't happen at all, and don't get me started on Crypto Currencies and NFT's! It's not good for my blood pressure.

Another thing that amazes me is the vast and growing number of people who seem to make a living from posting stuff on-line, although I have no idea how this counts as employment. They refer to themselves and each other as Influencers, but I foresee a time when we have perhaps a whole generation who want to be Influencers and nobody who is willing to pay good money to be influenced. Unless they are all just going to influence each other, but I'm not sure how that would work. It would surely be like circle time in a primary school.

Now you may be thinking that all this sounds a little wistful; that I suffer from FOMO: Fear Of Missing Out in some way. You see – I do have some of the jargon, but this could not be further from the truth. I have everything I need or want technology-wise. I don't need silent vehicles chasing me up the road; I don't need rockets or bullet-proof windows.

And yet I am as much a slave to technology as the next person. There is a lovely man in the village who comes to the rescue whenever repairs to my laptop are needed, and that's all I need. He has my laptop at the moment. It started behaving badly, just scrolling and scrolling and refusing to stop, no matter what I did until I switched it off. I suspect it just got fed up with being overworked. It was happy to play cards and look at funny stories, but nothing else; it seemed it didn't want to write books and stories just at the moment. And how do I feel? I feel as if my right arm has been chopped off.

I'm typing this story on my geriatric desktop, Methuselah, in Windows 7. I swear that this machine must be driven by steam power, it's so slow and there's an aperture in the side that was probably originally for a crank handle, you know, like on the earliest cars to get them started.

And it got me thinking. What if an electric car behaved as my laptop has done and did that on the motorway? Took offence at the way I was driving it and just went on and on moving, refusing to stop, what then?

No, for the most part you can keep these new-fangled innovations, and a happy Techno Numpty I shall remain.

Rainbow Bridge

Pixie had been a beautiful dog, a rescue whose previous owner had died as an old man, and whom Phoebe had rehomed because the dog was old and slow, as was she.

The rescue centre, she felt, was very generous and having Pixie's best interests at heart, offered Phoebe help should she need it, with future vet bills. They did this apparently for all their senior dogs – those aged ten years and above, as an incentive for people to rehome these less appealing canines. Phoebe had thanked them and said that she would approach them if necessary. She was not prepared to say that she was very comfortably off, and that other rehomers were surely in more need of the charity's funds.

She and Pixie strolled sedately round the neighbourhood twice every day, and three times if the weather was cool enough. Either he obligingly matched his pace to hers, or they were perfectly matched, and for three years Pixie rarely left Phoebe's side. When her aches and pains, or severe weather made walking impossible, her son would walk Pixie until she felt better. As the pair of them walked, they met friends old and new, both canine and human. Some of the younger dogs they met were rather too boisterous for Pixie. He solved this problem by simply lying down wherever he was and watching them gambol around him whilst their owners talked.

And then, just two days before Phoebe's eighty second birthday Pixie passed away. He was fourteen years old. For the first time since she was six years old Phoebe was without a dog in the family, but at her age she had decided that it would be unfair to bring home another dog; one that she may soon not be able to look after properly. She hated coming in to an empty house, even though sometimes the greetings across the years had been over-effusive. On one occasion her Labrador Sampson had been so pleased to see her home that he had knocked her clean off her feet and her shopping bag had hit the floor with a thud. A carton of juice split and Phoebe found herself sitting in the hall in a sticky puddle whilst Sampson tried to pretend it was nothing to do with him as he surreptitiously slurped orange juice off the parquet. But she was much younger then and better able to weather such tumbles. If that had happened more recently she could have been sitting there for hours.

The vet came and took Pixie away, to do what needed to be done, and Phoebe found the house intolerably quiet. Pixie had not been a noisy dog, but he was just always there. She even missed the whiffly little snorts and grunts Pixie had made in his sleep;

dreaming of cats, or chasing sheep perhaps.

She sat in the armchair where he had been used to lie at her feet, until she could stand it no longer and with a tear trickling down her cheek she packed up Pixie's dog bed, his clean blanket and his food and water bowls. She would take them to the rehoming centre, or perhaps get her son to do it. She felt so very tired, and couldn't face up to seeing all those dogs still looking for homes. Would she still go out on walks several times a day? Common sense said it would be a good idea to keep moving, but without her little shadow to meet and snuffle with other dogs, and people; her special friend who seemed to stop every five minutes to check what Phoebe called his pee-mails, it just wouldn't be the same.

She had missed all the dogs who had been her family over the years: Scooch, the snappy little terrier who had travelled to their home on her knee in the back of the family car, just before her seventh birthday, Jasper the soppy retriever who was afraid of his own shadow and everything else. She smiled as she recalled Scamp from Romania, a crazy mix of sheepdog with only one ear and a flattened foot, Polly a noisy Bedlington terrier who succumbed in the early days of the disease to Parvo virus, before it could be identified and treated. There were others whose names she could no longer recall, but they had all been loved in their day. They had all been her companions over the years and they had been special. Time passed by as Phoebe sat and remembered.

Her eighty second birthday dawned, yet still she sat and had not moved when her son arrived to take her out to lunch. Her son later recounted to his wife the shock of finding that his mother had passed away, so soon after the loss of her beloved dog, just sitting in her chair 'It was just as if she was hanging on until Pixie didn't need her anymore,' he told her.

*

Meanwhile Phoebe woke and found herself standing straighter than she had done for years. She was pain-free as she walked unaided down a long straight lane of overhanging trees with Mimosa-smelling flowers. Towards her scampered a group of dogs, led by Pixie, who was younger and bouncing along with a sure-footed Scamp beside him. Behind them was Polly, flanked by Scooch and Jasper. Following on to meet Phoebe were other dogs she had known: her aunt's Pomeranian and her mother's Airedale, in fact all the dogs that had meant something in her life: the neighbours' enormous German Shepherd, and her cousin's golden retriever guide dog. Every dog she had ever known and loved was streaming back along the lane as far as she could see, and hurrying to greet her.

'I expected heaven to be pearly gates and perhaps golden pillars,' she said to them as they rolled and played in ecstacy at her feet in a huge canine scrum, 'I should have known that heaven would be filled with dogs like this.'

First Love

Larry sat on the train platform, waiting. The noticeboard said that the train was running forty five minutes late; not long enough to go anywhere or do anything else, but just sit and wait. He took a swig of his takeaway coffee and looked around.

At a nearby bench sat a couple; a woman and, closer to Larry, largely shielding her from his view, was a young man. As he watched, the young man turned his head so that his face was visible and Larry nearly dropped his coffee. For he was looking at the image of himself as a young man. What was that German word he had heard? Doppelganger? Somebody who looked exactly the same as him. He sat transfixed, unable to move his gaze away.

The likeness was uncanny. He had the same reddish hair, already receding rather at the temples, as Larry's own had done at that sort of age. His jaw was lantern and his face had a perpetually tanned looked.

His eyes were hooded, redeemed by the crinkling lines evident as he spoke, and particularly noticeable each time he smiled, which he did often.

The young man turned to say something to the woman, who shook her head, then he stood up and walked past Larry on his way to the coffee vendor. He was very tall, maybe even taller than Larry, and his gait, a sort of simian lope, was like Larry's too. Now that he had moved out of the way, Larry could clearly see the woman he was with. Seeming to sense that she was being watched, she looked in his direction, then quickly looked away again, with no sign of recognition.

Larry caught his breath. It was Hope. They say that you never forget your first love, and Larry had certainly never forgotten Hope. It must be twenty years since he had last seen her, when he went off to London to university and she stayed behind in Devon. At that point it was already as if their lives were destined to go in different directions.

Larry thought about the time that had passed between university and now. Now he was the proprietor and Director of Waite's Recruitment Agency. Larry Waite had worked hard, starting the business from nothing and was now worth a lot of money. He loved his work, and it had always kept him busy but he had given no time to commit to getting married, and he had no children.

Or had he? Looking carefully at this young man he noted again the same jawline, the same colouring, and eyes of a piercing blue, although his own were now rather faded. He was suddenly certain. This was his son. Larry was seventeen when he met

Hope, and they were what he called *an item* for over six months, until university entrance and a change of city killed the budding relationship. It seemed that Hope must have been pregnant when he went off to university; certainly she was not around when he came home. His attention was focused on travelling and then setting up the business, but he had been sure that he would have noticed her if she had been living where they were both brought up; he wouldn't have forgotten his first love, his only love. He had quizzed his mother, who said that she and her family had moved away over the summer when he first went to university.

    As he looked intently at the young man now he became more and more convinced that this was indeed his own son, born to Hope after she moved away, and never acknowledged as his. Both of Larry's parents had died quite young, and there was nobody now who he could ask. Except Hope herself, and here she was, right here. But could he do that? Could he go up to her and reintroduce himself? Who did this young man think his father was? Would he be outraged or delighted? Could he say to this young stranger that he thought he was his dad? Of course he couldn't.

    But nor could he just let Hope go, with maybe neither of them knowing the truth. He planned his words, going through possibilities in his head. What if she didn't recognise him? She had glanced his way once and not registered any sort of recognition. Perhaps he had changed so much in the intervening years.

He followed the young man to the coffee vendor, hoping that he didn't look suspicious. Standing close to him he could see that he had the same thick neck, with gingery hair growing low over attached earlobes, just like Larry's own. He remembered that Hope and he had often laughed about his attached earlobes, saying it was a good job it was him and not her who had that, because he would have struggled to wear the ornate earrings that his first love favoured.

'I said yes, sir. How can I help you?'

Larry realised that the boy had been served and had moved away. It was the server who was challenging him for his order.

'Sorry, just a white coffee please,' he said and took it back to the same bench. There were now just a few minutes more to wait for his train. If he was going to challenge Hope, and he felt that he must, then he must do it now. He could at least get a phone number and keep in touch.

As his train snaked around the end of the platform towards them, he stood and moved towards the bench where the couple, mother and son were also now standing up and gathering their belongings.

He threw his empty coffee cup in the bin and went and stood in front of his first love. As he opened his mouth to speak he heard a voice calling behind him. It was someone who had just alighted from the newly arrived train.

'Hope! Hope! How lovely of you to come and meet me. And Jonathan too, this is a real treat. I didn't know you were home this week, Son.'

Son? Larry was about to turn and start to concoct some sort of explanation, when the man bustled past him, nudging him gently out of the way. He swept up Hope in his arms, until she pushed him playfully away, 'You daft thing. You've only been gone three days. It's good to see you though.'

The man turned for a bear hug with the younger man and Larry had the chance to get a good look at him. He was identical to the younger man, the red hair, the thick neck, the ears – everything.

As Hope gathered her two men on either side of her, Larry stood back. Of course it made sense that if Larry was Hope's type, the kind of man she was physically attracted to, then so too would be this man, so similar in appearance were they.

He boarded the train that the stranger had just left, half relieved that he had not made a fool of himself, and half sad that the young man was not indeed the offspring of himself and Hope – his first love.

I Would Walk Five Hundred Miles

It wasn't anywhere near five hundred miles of course, but in the heat we've had these last two days it sure felt like it.

I started this job two weeks ago. Just two weeks and already I was wondering if I'd made a dreadful mistake. I'd spent these first two weeks accompanying various drivers on their deliveries and quickly come to some conclusions.

Firstly, while the late shift suited my lifestyle, it had produced issues. I saw that the customers opting for evening delivery timeslots fell into two main categories. The first are busy working people, too busy to shop *in real life,* as I think of it. They are often tired, short-tempered, brusque and demanding. I dread delivering a bottle of spirits that the picker hasn't dealt with properly and which still has its security tag attached. You would think the world had ended. Such customers are not happy if they don't have immediate access to their booze. It makes me wonder how they get through the working day without it.

The other thing about this group is that they don't half moan about substitutions, and of course it's the delivery driver that gets the fall-out. I must agree sometimes. I know the pickers have to be quick but I wonder what they are thinking of. Last week one customer had ordered *four ripe and ready avocados,* but the picker had substituted beetroot – yes beetroot! The customer was not happy. I watched as my colleague diplomatically explained to her that without avocados in stock we couldn't fulfil her order. We would take the beetroot back and refund her. She knew all this of course. She just wanted somebody to grumble at, and she still wasn't happy, just moaning about *how would she cope without her avocados?* It took me all my time not to laugh at her, she was such a drama queen.

The second group to go for these later slots are pensioners. They're around all day but go for the evening slots because they are cheaper, even if it means sometimes unpacking their shopping in the dark. And they take forever to unpack, sometimes checking every single item against their original list, watching out for bashed tins and bruised vegetables, checking Best Before dates, before they can move on.

Officially the late shift finishes at ten o'clock but of course I have to keep going till all the deliveries are made. And that policy doesn't suit some customers either obviously, because if it goes past ten o'clock there are often complaints that it's past their bedtime.

Well, that was awful. It's roasting hot today, the first nice weather we've had for ages. I've just made a delivery to a third floor flat. I don't know how many of them are in the household but I suspect that they don't have everything delivered, just the heavy stuff. Today, there was a dozen bottles of lemonade, a giant box of washing powder and a big sack of dog food along with loads of other stuff.

Of course, wouldn't you know it, when I got to the entry hall of the flats the lift was out of order and I had to make six, yes six, journeys up three flights of stairs to complete the delivery. Have you seen that Specsavers advert on TV with the Proclaimers soundtrack? Where the delivery guy takes something big and heavy up to a high flat, only for the woman who answers the door to point out that he's come to the wrong block? It was a bit like that, except that there's nothing wrong with my eyesight and I had to do it six times over. I'm not sure I can cope with this job, not if it's going to be like this.

*

I arrived at my next customer, my face as red as a tomato. As I lifted the first of her crates out of the van she saw my face, dripping with sweat.

'Oh, you poor man,' she said, pointing to a bench next to her front door, 'sit yourself down for a minute. I'll get you a cold drink and you have that while I unpack this first crate.'

Ignoring my protests she disappeared into her bungalow, and came out with a small can of lemonade, cold from the fridge, and a facecloth that she had soaked in cold water then rung out. In the meantime I had unloaded her other groceries from the van and then sat down as instructed. I could feel the beetroot colour draining out of my face as I sat in the shade and relaxed, the facecloth draped across the back of my neck, which felt on fire. I wiped the can across my forehead, then popped open the ring-pull – nectar.

I must have closed my eyes for a second or two because the next thing I noticed the lady was standing in front of me and the remaining crates were all empty.

'Feeling better?' she asked, sitting down beside me, 'I thought you were going to peg out on me.'

I told her about the flats, and that I hadn't brought nearly enough liquid to drink through the shift.

'It must be awkward,' she said, 'if you drink too much I suppose there's a danger of constantly needing the loo. If you're delivering here, and I hope you'll become our regular driver, then you're welcome to use our facilities,' she blushed a pretty pink, 'We always have these little cans in the fridge in case the grandchildren visit. Perhaps you could ask some of the more experienced drivers how they cope when it's this hot.'

She handed over a further chilled drink, and refused my offer to pay for it. She had also rinsed out the facecloth again, and popped it into a plastic bag with a few ice cubes.

'Hopefully, these will help cool you down a bit for the rest of the shift.'

I waved goodbye to her and made my way to my next customer. I think I will stick with this job and take her advice. I'll ask the other drivers how they cope in the heat.

Hopefully she'll be one of my regulars, as she's quite restored my faith in human nature.

Drippy Deluge

It's not always an exciting story mine, but I suspect yours isn't either. Most of us just plug away from day to day with very occasional spikes of really good stuff happening to us. Let me tell you a little of my life story and you can be the judge. I say life story, but that is a bit of a misnomer. I don't have a life which, like yours, began with a birth and ended with death. Rather I have a continuum of experience. Stick around and I'll explain what I mean.

Rumour has it that in London when people drink a glass of water it has already been through eight other people, I'm not sure that's true, but what is true is that we never die. We are the ultimate recyclers, existing in a closed system called the water cycle. Oh, I forgot to introduce myself. My name is Drippy Deluge, although I'm hardly ever seen alone. I am a drop of water.

Some background information: all water exists

as a solid, a liquid or as a gas – well we all know that, but for a drop of water like me, it makes life very interesting, because nothing stays the same and even though there is a prescribed cycle, that in itself is flexible. Not that I am alive in the way that you are alive; I have microscopic creatures living in me, but this story is about me and my chums, not the little creatures. I have existed since the beginning of the earth – I know! Crazy isn't it? And nobody knows just how long that is. But that's what we mean by a closed system.

Basically, if we say, for example, that the cycle starts by us gushing out of your tap, then we would be poured down the drain into the sewers, who flush us out to sea. When it's hot the sea and other surface waters evaporate up into the sky only to fall eventually as rain. This rain is used to fill reservoirs and from there to feed the taps in your homes. See? And so the cycle is complete. It does seem to me that, however I spend my time on earth, I do spend quite a large percentage of time in the sewers and in the sea, which has to be the least pleasant part of our cycle.

It would be very boring for me and for the other water droplets if that was the limit of our adventures. In fact we can go all over the world, and see all sorts of things. I can almost guarantee that I've travelled further than you have! We can go under the surface of the world as well; think about caves you may have been in and seen water pools and stalactites and stalagmites. These are all basically water. We can soak into the ground and stay there for years. Many years ago, I got stuck in one of these caves, and it was only when a couple of children started splashing about with their hands in the edge of the water, that I was brought up to the surface, splashed up as a droplet on the little boy's hair.

I love it when children interact with us. I remember one time a little girl of about four years old was on a winter walk with her mum. Water began to fall in the form of hailstones, it was so cold. This little girl began scooping up handfuls of the hailstones and was putting them in her pocket. When her mother asked what on earth she was doing, she said she wanted to take them into school on the Monday for the nature table!

I was surprised how many watery words there are; drops and drips and puddles and lakes and ice and taps and so on, but then it seems that we are the most important thing that there is. In.The.Whole.World! It's quite a claim that we can make.

There are lots of other worlds and planets out there and some of them may have some water, but if they don't, then nothing can live on them, no plants, people, animals, nothing. So without me and my kind, you and your kind would not be here. Just think about that!

Allow me to tell you a little bit about what I do and the places I have seen. It's hard to know where to begin. Because of the water cycle we are never born, and we never die. We just exist in all sorts of forms. People and animals drink water of course, but we're also used to make into anything that's wet – lemonade and fruit juice are particularly nice, yummy; engine oil and weed killer not so nice, but we don't have a choice we just go where we are sent. I spent some time in a dialysis machine once, helping to clean out somebody's kidneys – it's an important job that we have. We are also used in all sorts of manufacturing processes. Some of these need special pure water, with everything removed – dust, chemicals everything. We are clean enough then to be used in things like cosmetics, drugs, and for cleaning metal where a really smooth finish is needed like car bodies or white goods.

    I think one of my earliest memories was one exciting adventure after I was piped out to sea from a sewage plant. It was a very warm day and I evaporated, floating up into the sky to become one of those little fluffy clouds that you people can see. It was one of the best periods. This country is beautiful when seen from above. The nearest you people can get to it is from a plane or a drone, but there's nothing like being buffeted on the open breeze, along with thousands and thousands of other water droplets. Then of course the clouds got buffeted together and we become more and more heavy with water until in the end we rain down onto the earth. That first time I can remember I landed in a dog bowl that someone had put outside their front gate. A dog drank me, and it was very warm and sort of fuzzy in its tummy. Then a person took the dog out for a walk and it did a wee up the side of a lamp-post. A man cleaning his car turned his hosepipe our way and flushed us all down into a gulley alongside the footpath. I didn't know where we were going, but we ended up in a river. It was only a little river and some of the other droplets who'd been there before called it a tributary. We were all swept away through fields, along the edge of a football ground and between some houses. We stayed lovely and cool all the way to join the bigger river that swept more sedately along. Eventually we got to the sea and the process started again.

One time I fell as hail into a canal. Hail is different because it is cold, hard, and on that occasion it got blown in the wind, until a whole heap of us piled up like little stones on the ice that formed the surface of the water. Someone had made some holes in the ice in places, so the fishes could breathe, and so the ducks and other birds could get to drink, which was kind of them. We stayed piled up there for nearly two weeks, it was so cold. Then the water thawed out and the surface rose so high that it flooded right over the overflow sluice gates and I ended up in that same river and off to the sea again.

This time was different though, there were some very unusual wind currents about, and I found myself in a totally different country in a fire bowser in a remote American township being used to damp down fires and save the lives of people whose house was on fire. Then I was swept along the sewers into a lake and the next thing I knew I was putting out another fire, this time by gushing out of a fire hydrant early the next morning. It's a very strange tickly feeling when you get shot out a huge gun onto a dry fire, very tickly. Whatever I'm involved with, I nearly always end up in the sewers at some stage. I must say that sewers in one country smell much like those in another, none of them pleasant, but we're not usually in them too long before washed out to sea in amongst cleaner water, ready to start on our next cycle.

One early clear memory of mine that I mentioned is of falling, falling and landing in a bowl that was filling up with loads of water, all gushing with me from a kitchen tap. It was a bit scary dropping what seemed like a really long way, but I landed gently with loads of other water droplet, and some lovely-smelling soapy bubbles.

If you ask me which was my most exciting adventure though, it would have to be one time when I was in an inlet of the sea on a surf board, and I helped someone win the Olympics! Yes, I don't mean I could choose who won it, I was just one of millions of droplets of water in a bay that was used for some of the sailing, swimming and diving events. I also helped with the boat race on the Thames one year when Oxford won, but that was less pleasant because our rivers these days are in a terribly mucky state. I couldn't see where I was even.

I've been used on gardens and farms, to water pretty plants, and also things that we can eat. I've been used in cooking to make food safe. I tell you, being boiled in a kettle or a pan doesn't half make you want to dance. I've travelled a couple of times to third world countries to help provide enough water for people who live in very hot, dry places and need wells digging to get down to the water table for clean drinking water. Sometimes, you know, we just soak into the ground to become groundwater or to fill aquifers, or eventually have to be pumped out of mines; we just never know from one day to the next. We might be in a milking shed, or the basis of a log flume, or in a washing machine. I've been in cans of Red Bull and bottles of alcohol, not always pleasurable experiences.

Some of the stuff has been just fun though. I

mentioned bubbles before in a bowl for washing dishes, but also I've been used by children for blowing bubbles. I've also been with children in paddling pools, splash pools, played at bathtime with ducks and toys that float and pour and sprinkle. It's lovely now and then in little ones' baths to think that you are helping them to learn about water, but we're never there long before being sucked down the plughole and out, inevitably to the sea. Being underground in the sewers is the part I like least, but then when the sea evaporates we become clouds again, and rain down onto the earth. The whole cycle thing continues all the time.

The best time to have been up in the clouds is when it's been really dry for ages, and the earth looks parched. You people look weary, and if I am able to be part of that first proper downpour for ages then it's wonderful. I've seen people just standing outside their houses, (sometimes with very few clothes on) just soaking up the rain, they are so glad to see us; and the flowers seem to turn up their faces in readiness. It makes me feels very much appreciated, and compensates for some of the less pleasant journeys I have to make, such as down the lavatory.

There are so many things I could tell you about us, and so many dozens of watery words, but I'll just leave you with a few thoughts.

To make a single pair of jeans, right from growing and watering the cotton plants and the whole process, it takes about seven and a half thousand litres of water. Amazing!

To make a single cup of tea, with milk and one spoonful of sugar takes fifty two litres of water. Yes, as much as that – to grow the tea bushes, water for the cows to produce milk and growing the sugar, as well as the actual water you boil in the kettle.

So you need to look after water and treasure it, not waste it. You need water more than water needs you.

Happy Landings

Jenna had never really enjoyed flying. She didn't dislike or fear it enough to feel the need for help or therapy, and not enough for it to actually stop her travelling by plane when she really wanted to go somewhere, but she didn't enjoy it. Having seen the burned out wreck of the Boeing 737 at Manchester Airport from 1985 she had read that take-off and landing were the most dangerous parts of the journey. That made sense, and she had always been happier once they were actually airborne, until it was time to begin the descent, when the jitters began again. The sensation of being above the clouds, or seeing the earth spread beneath them like a patchwork quilt was always fascinating, but still, she didn't find it a comfortable experience.

When their only child was still quite small they felt able to go abroad again after a gap of a few years, and decided to spend a week in Gibraltar. They didn't want to go too far on their first holiday abroad with a small child, and the flight from Gatwick took less than three hours. They were able to book one that meant they would land in the afternoon.

Before the days of ubiquitous Google Maps, Jenna had not had time to examine closely the geography of The Rock. She knew about the Barbary apes, the World War Two tunnels under the Rock, at Hays Level, and the underground hospital built when most of the civilian population was evacuated. That summed up Jenna's knowledge about Gibraltar, which was perhaps as well. They had also planned a day trip by boat, across the Strait of Gibraltar to Tangier in Morocco.

The flight was smooth, and Jenna's attention was taken up with their son, until the pilot's voice came over the speaker system to announce that they would shortly be landing at Gibraltar Airport, seats should be put in the upright position, trays put away, and all the usual announcements that Jenna had heard many times before.

But as the plane began to lose altitude the sun was beginning to set and all she could see out of the window was water. Where on earth was the airport? Where was the runway? And then as they banked for their final approach she saw it and her heart dropped. The airport boasted just one runway, and it looked incredibly short in comparison with the one they had taken off from in London. Jenna was terrified. How on earth was the plane they were on going to stop on such a short runway? She tried to tell herself that many planes had landed there before, including some carrying friends who had holidayed on The Rock, but panic doesn't recognise logic.

They did land safely, the approach being made from West to East, with only water was visible on either side of the plane until after the wheels had touched down and the plane began taxiing towards the airport building. Once they had stopped, before the doors were even opened the pilot announced the need to cross a road to reach the terminal building and advised caution, even though the road would be closed to traffic during the landing or take-off of planes. Jenna looked in horror at her partner. They disembarked and made their way across to the building, Jenna glad to have her little son to hold on to, hoping that her fear hadn't shown itself to him.

As the week wore on, for Jenna there was worse to come with no chance to avoid information about the Rock during the week's holiday. A brochure in the hotel bedroom contained a map, which Jenna looked at and then had to sit down. She saw that the road they had needed to walk across to reach the airport terminal, was Winston Churchill Avenue, the only access road across the border between Gibraltar and Spain. There is now also a tunnel under the border, but Jenna's experience predates this by many years. So their plane had landed and taxied across a main highway. She read that the runway was just over seventeen hundred metres long, just over half the length of the one at Gatwick. Mesmerised, she was driven to read on, and saw that there were hazards for pilots approaching the single runway. The rock rose a majestic four hundred metres immediately to the south, and the unique geography meant that cross-winds could be treacherous.

It haunted her all week. Her husband had found the whole journey and landing experience exhilarating and wondered aloud what the return journey would be like. Jenna felt sick with apprehension. Arriving at the airport on the afternoon of their departure, she wondered whether it would have been better to arrive in the dark so that she would have remained in ignorance, but the pride that the locals had in their extreme geography and their unusual airport would have made it difficult to avoid this information.

Walking across the main road once again to board the plane, Jenna could clearly see the whole of the runway. To the east it seemed to lie perilously close to the south edge of the sheer rock, and to the west even more scarily, at least a third of its short length projected beyond the natural contours of the land into the sea.

Taking off was even more terrifying to Jenna than landing had been. As soon as the rock was cleared and the plane accelerating, the end of the runway seemed to approach so quickly, and there would, she thought, be no scope to abort a flight. Impossible to turn to right or left as there was nothing there, just the sea.

The take-off and journey were uneventful. Once safely landed back at Gatwick, Jenna's husband asked whether she had enjoyed the holiday. Did she not think Gibraltar well worth visiting?

Indeed it was she agreed, and she would like to go back one day, but next time perhaps they might go via car through Spain, and across the border that way rather than fly?

The Tree Feller

The Derness family, Alasdair, his wife Isabel along with their children, Bee and Olli, lived near Orkney with their boxer dog Fire. As he prepared to leave the house that morning, Alasdair looked in on his younger son, tucked up in bed but resisted the temptation to give him a goodbye kiss. Olli was a light sleeper and it could be difficult for Isabel if he woke up and was upset. As Al closed the bedroom door behind him with a gentle *thunk* he thought he'd got away with it. Then he heard it, an audible gasp, encapsulating the angst stored up in his young son's heart before the tears began, Olli lacked the ability to hide his feelings. His heart was always clearly visible as he wore it on his sleeve at all times. This time though it was serious; for the first time since Olli was born, Al Derness may be away for much longer than he had been before.

The previous evening he had sat down his two

children and talked seriously to them. They had changed into their pyjamas ready for bed, 'You must work hard at school, and be good for Mummy while I'm away. Hopefully it will only be for a couple of days.'

'Where are you going?' Bee wanted to know.

'I'm going to talk to a man about a new job.'

'But you have a job, Pop. Why do you need a new one?' Olli's lip was beginning to quiver.

'What's up Olli?'

'Me and Larry were talking at school. He said you might be leaving us because you are going to work a long way away.' The tears were flowing in earnest now.

'Pop, Larry's not right is he? You're not going to leave us? Please!'

'Of course I'm not leaving you, silly sausage.' Al put his arm round the little boy, 'Let me tell you what will be happening.

'You see, the job that I have been doing has mostly been taken over by machines now, and soon I won't be needed there anymore, so I'm going to talk to someone I knew a long time ago, who is looking for a lumberjack on his estate. It's what my Pop did for a living and I often used to go to work with him, so I know quite a lot about it.'

'Aren't machines doing chopping down trees down too, Pop? I saw a programme about it.'

'Yes they are Bee, but the big machines are really being used only on the really big plantations over on the western mainland. Here around Orkney because it's very exposed to the North Sea, and it's very windy, the few tree growing estates much smaller. Big logging machinery won't fit and would be too expensive to move here. It would also be too expensive for the small woodsmen. They want to stop depending on the electricity that this big machinery needs, and go back to the old ways of using manpower.'

'Or womanpower,' Bee championed gender equality at every opportunity.

'Of course, although you need to be very strong, so it does seem generally to suit men better.'

'Will you have to fly there to see the man, on a plane?' Olli made flying movements with his arms.

'Will you be the big boss? The head man?' his daughter wanted to know.

Al laughed. 'So many questions,' he answered them in turn,

'I won't be the big boss, but I would be a supervisor. Buses run past the main office for this new company every hour, so a plane won't be necessary. Anyway it's only about two and a half hours away. But that's just the office; the plantation with the trees is the one nearer to the airport, so that's not far at all.'

'I thought you and Mummy said that when school finished for the summer we could go away on holiday.' Bee was near to tears.

'Aye, we did, but I need to get this job sorted out first. My old job will owe me some holiday pay when I leave, so the plan is to have a little gap before I start the new job, just a week or two, and we'll use that gap to go on holiday. Okay? Now, it's late. Time for cocoa, kisses goodnight and snuggle down for sleep, okay? If I get the job, then I'll show you where it will be on the map. Leave it for now and settle down.'

Later, over a whisky and soda apiece, Isabel Derness asked Alasdair how the children had taken the news. They had agreed that Alasdair would tell them on his own as he would be better prepared to answer any questions, 'Did you have a nice chat?'

'It was nice, darling. Yes. They seemed quite upbeat once I'd answered some questions, and cocoa always helps.'

'I just hope it works out. Otherwise we might have to uproot the children from school and their friends to move nearer to one of the big tree plantations.'

'Hopefully it won't come to that.'

Al was away for less time than he had anticipated. His new boss wanted him to start as soon as possible, and allocated one of the office staff, Holly, to go through the procedures with him.

After working his notice with his old employer, he, Isabel, the children and the dog took off for a couple of weeks' holiday, and he took up his new post on their return.

A strange little tale I think you'll agree, but can you find the secret that it holds? There are the names of seventeen different trees hidden in the text. How many can you find? The answer is on the Acknowledgements page at the end of this book.

Bobby's Birthday

It was only a tiny charity shop tucked away behind the cathedral at the top of the city's main street. With little passing footfall and no signage to speak of, the young couple weren't surprised that they hadn't stumbled across it before.

Their little son, Bobby, stood and gazed in awestruck wonder in at the tiny shop window, a window dominated by a bright green ride-on toy tractor with trailer attached. The only apparent problem with the vehicle seemed to be its upright exhaust pipe which, instead of being tall and shiny metal was cracked and broken. Other than a few bumps and scratches and it needing a good clean, there was little else wrong.

Little Bobby adored tractors: from full sized ones they passed in the fields and on the country roads at harvest time, through the ride-on ones he came across in play parks and activity centres, down to model ones by Dinky and Corgi. For his upcoming birthday Nanny and Pa had bought him a farmyard scene in which to keep his favourite toys, and his birthday card depicted a small boy with a big grin riding on a tractor very similar to that in the charity shop window.

It was a huge broken down yellow digger parked up at the side of a farm track that first started Bobby's interest in trucks and the like. Every time they walked past it, which was several times at least every week, he would ask whether he could play on it. It had to be explained that, wrecked though it was, it belonged to somebody and was not there to be played on. Also the amount of rust, and oil and particularly the broken glass from the windows and windscreen, which looked as if they had been used for target practice, made it unsafe. Nevertheless each time they went down the track he would walk slowly and unsteadily around the vehicle, enchanted by its size, its colour and what fun he suspected it to be capable of.

This last he knew because he had the modern Dinky equivalent, and whenever the weather allowed he would take it out, with a few other vehicles, to play in the sandpit, loading its shovel, moving the sand, then tipping it out. This way he would spend hour after happy hour.

In the charity shop Bobby's Mum and Dad exchanged a smile and a wink over his head. When Mum took Bobby and his brother and sister into a nearby café, his Dad doubled back and spoke to the person manning the shop.

'We'll need it for Bobby's birthday a week on

Saturday,' Dad explained, but I'm not sure where we're going to store it. He will be three that day and I don't want him to see it come home with us beforehand. With the four of us in the car, we won't be able to hide it.'

'No problem.' The man immediately removed the tractor and trailer from the shop window and they agreed a price, which Bobby's Dad paid. 'I'll hang on to it until the Saturday morning if you like, or I can drop it off at your house on Friday evening if it suits you. I live to the north of the city and it's not far out of my way. See, I'll put this *SOLD* notice on it and put it in the storeroom at the back.' He handed over his business card, 'That's my number. You make your plans, and let me know what's best for you.'

On the morning of his birthday Bobby came downstairs to the strains of his brother and his parents singing *Happy Birthday*. At just three years old he wasn't entirely sure what a birthday was all about, except his brother had one just a few weeks before, and it seemed to involve presents and cake, and some hot candles that he was not allowed to touch. His Mum had asked him what he wanted to do on his birthday and he opted to go to the local ice cream farm where, of course they had tractors and diggers as well as animals.

'Fine,' said his mum as his dad picked up his phone to take photographs, 'Just go and wait in the living room while we get ready.'

In the middle of the living room was a big parcel. It was wrapped in Paw Patrol paper, which Bobby ripped off with a bit of help from his older brother. Inside was the green tractor and trailer, which he found just perfect for riding round and round the garden, the trip to the ice cream farm forgotten. Fortunately his mum had stocked up beforehand.

The man at the charity shop, true to his word, had kept it safe and delivered it, but he had done much, much more. The broken exhaust pipe had been fixed and made safe for little fingers, the dirt and scratches had all been polished out, and it glistened as it would have done when it was new. Best of all were the number plates. The shopkeeper had painted the background to these black, before sticking self-adhesive numbers and letters onto them that made no doubt as to who owned the tractor. The number plates clearly read *BOBBY 3*.

The perfect birthday present for a little boy.

From Darkest Peru

'I missed the meeting, I missed the meeting. I don't know what's happening!'

'If you hadn't rolled off the table onto the floor, you wouldn't have missed the meeting and you'd know. Mind you, you are a bit of a roly-poly shape aren't you?'

'Just cos you're skinny in the middle. Anyway why are we all being put in boxes?'

'Stop panicking. It's what happens to you all now. You're going on such an adventure. You're well-padded in the boxes, nice and cosy. Then you're going to be flown miles and miles away on a huge aeroplane to England, and eventually you'll end up as someone's lunch.'

'What? Someone's lunch! I don't want to be eaten, I want to stay here.'

'And do what? Everybody else is going. You can chat on the plane, and even in the shop while you're waiting to be bought, as long as the customers don't hear you.'

'Can I at least leave this big stone behind? It's really heavy.'

'No. All avocados have a big stone in their tummy, yours is no different than anyone else's. Stop moaning.'

'I don't think I want to be eaten. It doesn't sound much fun.'

'It'll be fine. Otherwise you'd be no use for anything. It's the reason why all you avocados are grown, so that you can be sold for food.'

'Like slavery you mean?'

'Hmm, not exactly slavery, no. But if you were to get your way and stay here, you would just lie on the forest floor on your own and rot.'

'Well, that doesn't sound much fun. The box and the aeroplane it is.'

I hadn't realised it would be so dark, and so noisy on that plane. The boxes we were in were all labelled fragile, so we weren't being thrown about too much, and, after a long ride in the back of a chilled lorry, here we are now at a shop. I must say we've been arranged very prettily, all facing the same way, and we've all been given a badge. It reads, hang on a minute, I need to twist round a bit, it reads *Finest Avocados, Product of Peru*. Peru! That's where Paddington Bear came from. It worked out okay for him coming to England; he got to meet the Queen and have tea with her. I wonder if we'll be meeting royalty, perhaps they like avocados.

Well! What an exciting morning I've had. Two of us were picked up and placed in a shopping basket, then wobbled over something that flashed a light and bleeped at us – not sure what all that was about. Then we were put in a different bag and brought to somebody's kitchen. We're not in the fridge, so it's a lot warmer than that aeroplane, but we're sitting on a pretty dish on the kitchen worktop. I don't think it's where the king lives, although it's a really nice place.

One of the people in the shop saw us in the shopping basket and said, *Oh, lovely avocados, half for a face-pack, half for a sandwich.* I'm not sure I want to be either, but really the face pack idea sounds gross. It's what happens afterwards that's worrying; I don't think anyone would want to eat us then.

Ooh, that person just came and squeezed me! That's a bit personal. I could have told her that that's not the best clue to ripeness; she should have flipped my little cap off. If I'm green underneath, then I'm ripe, if not I need to go back on the dish for another couple of days, preferably with an over ripe banana for company. Luckily for her I am ripe, and she's just cut me completely in two! She's taken my jacket off and popped it in a bucket marked *Compost.*

Being sliced up and then mashed wasn't much fun, but the knife tickled rather nicely when I was spread on toast. Oh my word, what's that? Sorry if I sound a bit muffled now, but she's plonked something on top of me, it's a bit slimy and cool and damp. It's also a funny orange colour. The packet says *Smoked Salmon* and it does smell rather nice, if a bit strong.

I've just noticed that there's a smaller person watching her do all this.

'What happens to the stone from the avocado's middle, Mummy?' she asked. I was glad she did, because I was rather wondering that myself. I grew from that stone, and felt quite attached to it.

The bigger person thought for a minute, 'Go and get me four cocktail sticks from the dining room sideboard,' she said to the smaller person, 'they're sharp. Be careful you don't stick them in your hands.'

By the time the small person came back, the other one had made a second sandwich from my other half, overlaid with some more of the salmon. I'm getting to quite like that smell.

She put the sandwiches on plates, and pushed them to one side, then took the cocktail sticks from the smaller person. She took a glass vase from the cupboard, and stuck the four cocktail sticks into my stone, so that they stuck out on different sides. These she balanced across the top of the vase. She then used a little watering can to carefully fill the vase with water to just below the cocktail sticks, so that most of the stone was underwater.

'There,' she said, 'now we leave it. Every day or two we'll add water as the level drops, and each week we'll put in fresh water completely so that it doesn't go slimy.' She placed the vase on the window ledge in the sunshine.

'Now, we have our lunch,' she said.

So it rather looks as if this is where I part company from you. I'm glad I didn't leave my stone behind, and that it will live on. If they really look after it and keep it warm enough, it might even grow another avocado, like it grew me. They're ready to take their first mouthfuls now, so I'm going in! Whoopee, what an adventure!

Ben Springer's Story

My name is Michael and I was born in a deprived area of Birmingham in 1958. I'm standing in front of the mirror now putting on a tie, something I haven't done for a long time; but you have to make an effort for a funeral don't you? I'm kinda hoping that they ask me to speak a little about Ben. I hadn't spoken to him for years, but he comes up on my radar from time to time, with him being so well known now. He was born in the same year as me, in the same poor area of Birmingham, and I remember they were a big Caribbean family. There were eight children in all including Ben and his twin, although I'm afraid I've forgotten her name.

It wasn't a happy home life for Ben, who experienced, like a lot of others in that area, a great deal of racial abuse; even though the people in UK had been begging for Caribbean men to come and do the menial jobs that they themselves didn't want to do.

I experienced that myself. My dad had come over after seeing an advert for bus drivers. It wasn't just that for Ben though, he had it much worse.

Although he went to church every Sunday and made his wife and the kids go too, Ben's father was a violent man, especially towards his wife, the mother of his eight children. I don't know, of course, what went on behind closed doors and Ben never talked about it, but it was so bad that when Ben was ten his mother ran away from home, taking just Ben with her and they went into virtual hiding. I don't know why she took him out of all of them. Perhaps because he struggled with reading and writing, and she was worried for his future. I don't know. Now that I'm a parent and grandparent myself, I understand that it must have been a heartbreaking decision for a mother to make. Things must have been really bad. Once they had got away there was even less money and the two of them lived hand to mouth, but at least the violence at home stopped. It was at this early stage of our lives that I knew Ben best. He really struggled at school, couldn't concentrate, same as I couldn't, and we both got in with a bad crowd. We were bored, labelled as failures, and teachers said it was a way of getting attention. Ben's problems were different to that though, he struggled – really struggled with reading and writing – it just didn't make any sense to him.

He had a lovely singing voice I remember, and a great sense of rhythm. Since then I've read about him from time to time, even seen him on the television. Even with everything he had gone through he never lost his cheeky, toothy grin and I was proud to say that I had known him, and liked him very much, and I think that he liked me too.

*

  I'm Malcolm, and I'm an old man now, but still working. In fact I've had to take time off work for a funeral today, one I wouldn't have missed for the world, although it's terribly sad that Ben died at a comparatively young age. He had so much more to give. I heard about his death on the radio, and immediately I was whisked right back to the first day I saw him. I worked at the Young Offenders' Institute then where I had just started my first job, so I wasn't much older than a lot of the lads. I liked to think I helped them to settle in, and they knew that if things got too much they could always come and talk to me. Borstal they called it in those days, and it was more about punishment than rehabilitation, which was a shame because most of them weren't really bad lads, they'd just lost their way.
  I remember Ben was upset because he felt he'd let his mum down after she'd done so much to try and help him. He wasn't a bad lad really, just got in with a crowd like they do when they're bored and school doesn't seem to make much sense; he said he'd joined in with a gang because nobody likes to stand out and be taunted for being different. In that environment the peer pressure was too much to resist I suppose. He seemed to me to be very lost; he was thirteen, and after numerous punishments and sanctions, he'd finally been expelled from school.
  I tried to give him, and some of the others, a little pep talk but you know what kids are like – in one

ear and out the next. He was no different. I lost touch with him when he moved on from us, which was a shame, but working in that environment you sometimes hear about the lads who've passed through your hands. I was sorry to hear that he went on to have several more spells in Borstal, and that as an older teen he was imprisoned in an adult unit for affray and burglary. It's not a good environment for a vulnerable lad, I wondered whether he might come across characters in there that dragged him down even more.

That's not what I'd talk about at his funeral though if I was asked. I'd talk about his openness; about his fight always for the underdog, without losing his sense of humour. About his toothy smile, his love of animals, and his fight for those who, like him, had struggled with illiteracy growing up. That was what drove him later in life I think, that wish to help others.

*

I'm Joseph. I'm going to a funeral this afternoon. A fellow Rastafarian and good friend who is gone too soon and will be badly missed.

Benjamin was sixty-five when he died, but he still had so much more to do, so much more to give. I first met him soon after he moved from Birmingham to London, determined to free himself from the culture of gangs and crimes in which he had become involved.

I remember him telling me about his teenage life in Birmingham. By the age of fifteen his poetry had become well known among the local Caribbean and Asian communities, and one stand-out moment for him was a conversation with an elderly man who had seen his struggles and asked him what he wanted from life. When Ben told him that he really wanted to be a poet, the man gifted him an ancient typewriter; even back then almost a hundred years old, and today that machine can be seen in the Birmingham Museum, to whom Ben later donated it. Ben told me it was almost too heavy for him to lift, but he used it to improve his literacy, and wrote all of his early poetry on it.

Poetry, Rastafarianism and a will of iron became his salvation. He had realised that he would spend more and more time in prison, or even suffer an early death because of his gang-related, drug-related activities, and aged twenty two, he had left Birmingham to get away from the gangs with whom he was involved, and carve out a new life in London, which is where I met him.

It seems strange to say that his salvation lay in poetry, when he had a very limited ability in reading and writing, but he was passionate about sharing the spoken word, and with his melodic voice he shared his works through dub poetry; often setting his poems to reggae music. He had been able to engage with the youngsters in the Caribbean and Asian communities, even as a teenager and he was also extremely musical as well as a great advocate of support for oppressed communities. He became first a vegetarian and later a vegan, championing the cause of farmed animals. He was once asked if he found himself alone in a desert, with only a cow as potential food, what he would do.

He responded that he would look at what the cow ate, and eat that too. I'm not sure that would work, but he was certainly sincere in his intentions.

Life in London wasn't easy for Ben when I first knew him. He continued to be singled out because of his race, and I remember he was seriously assaulted during the 1981 Brixton riots, but was determined not to be beaten down by life. In 1994 his first book of poetry for children *Talking Turkeys* had to go into emergency reprint after 6 weeks of its first publication it was so popular, and it stayed at the top of the children's booklist for months. I am proud to consider him my friend.

*

My name's John and I am going to a funeral today. I first met Benjamin in 1998 when he was shortlisted for the Radio 4 Young Playwrights Festival Award, which he then went on to win. Like many young men, he treated himself on the back of his success, by buying a brand new BMW. Sadly he felt obliged to sell it very soon, after being stopped four times by the police in quick succession for no other reason than he looked as he did and that he was driving an expensive car.

I have followed his career keenly. In 1999 his first novel for teenagers, *Face*, was reviewed by Raymond Antrobus in the Guardian. Raymond had been given a copy of the book when he had just started attending a School for the Deaf.

"I remember reading the whole thing in one

go," Antrobus wrote, "I was very self-conscious about wearing hearing aids and I needed stories that humanised disability, as Face did. I was still struggling with my literacy at the time, and I understood Ben as someone who was self-taught and had been marginalised within the education system."

Something I really appreciated about my friend Ben was his openness. He was not one to shy away from discussing any topic, and two things particularly stand out for me.

The first was that Ben discussed his infertility quite openly. In part, it led to the breakdown of his first marriage. It meant that there were no offspring which was a great source of sadness to his first wife. Unfortunately Ben's significant prison record debarred them from adopting children. Friction about children contributed to the breakdown of that first marriage and led to their divorce in 2001.

The second point I think made me realise how genuine a person he was; how principled. Always the radical, he described himself as an anarchist and in 2003 he was offered and turned down an OBE, saying:

"I get angry when I hear that word empire. It reminds me of slavery, it reminds me of thousands of years of brutality. It reminds me of how my foremothers were raped and my forefathers brutalised."

His career and popularity went from strength to strength. He felt, in a way, that writing was overrated. He would explain it much better than I can, but his point was that once something was committed to paper it became immutable; it became fact. A case in point was fairy tales, which for centuries were shared verbally and which evolved with the telling. Once written down there was no more scope for them to evolve and develop. For this reason throughout his work he continued to emphasise the importance of the spoken word.

He was appointed as Professor of Poetry and Creative Writing at Brunel University, London in 2011 and we lost touch as I moved away, and Benjamin spent more and more time in China. He went on to marry again; a lovely woman he met in China. Qian Zheng and Benjamin first met in 2014 and married three years later.

*

I've been to the funeral of a colleague this afternoon. Sad, because he was only in his sixties when he died, but it was a celebration of a life well lived, and an example to us all; especially those born into poverty, crime, and violence. He was my colleague, a fellow lecturer at Brunel University, and Benjamin's was a real *rags to riches* story. On a television show broadcast in 2020 I watched as he spoke of a strip-search he had recently undergone at Heathrow Airport, based on nothing more than his appearance and where he was travelling from.

He tried always to teach the oral traditions of his heritage, a lot of which was handed down by word of mouth. On that same show he was asked what item he would like to be buried with. Without any hesitation he cited that very first typewriter, now well over a hundred years old. He wanted to be buried with it so that, as he said, *"When I'm decomposing I'm still composing."* It was typical of Benjamin's humour, and what endeared him to all sorts of people.

Sadly, a week ago Benjamin suffered a brain haemorrhage and died, aged 65 on 7th December 2023, being succeeded by his second wife Qian.

Many years before, when he converted to Rastafarianism, he had changed his name, so you probably won't have heard of Ben Springer, but will undoubtedly have heard of him in his new name. He was my friend Benjamin Zephaniah.

Going, Going, Gone

I need to buy stuff to furnish a flat; my own flat; my new flat. Aunty Cynthia suggested I go to an auction. She says that some people change their furniture preferences nearly as often as they change their socks, which made me giggle. I know she'd come with me if I asked her and I really wanted to ask her, but, as she said, sooner or later I have to stand on my own two feet. Socks, feet – it sounds as if I'm obsessed doesn't it? I'm not. It's just hard for me to stay grounded, but I must take a deep breath and keep focused.

I have given them my name and address. I hesitated over that, because at first I nearly gave them my new one, but of course I haven't changed everything over yet, my bank details and that. Of course anything that goes to Aunty Cynth's house, where I'm living now, she'll send or bring on to me, so hers is the safest for another week or two. I've got my paddle, and my number, to wave if I want to buy anything. It's number thirteen, which I hesitated about, but Aunty Cynth says that sometimes you just have to roll with it. I had to ask what she meant, and she said I mustn't focus on detail and think of the bigger picture. She told me that when I was cleaning the kitchen counters at her house for the third time one morning last week. I was just not sure whether I'd cleaned up all the milk that had dripped from the jug, and then there was the banana skin that had flopped out of the little compost bin in the corner.

Anyway I'm here now and the auction is going to start.

Some of this stuff must be real quality. Aunty Cynth told me not to forget that I need to add on commission and VAT to the price I actually agree to pay for anything. We worked out roughly how much that would be and I've jotted it down here, on the list of stuff I need to get. I've set myself a limit of how much I can afford to spend overall and I won't go over it by a penny. Aunty Cynth told me that I have some flexibility, not to let a piece I really want go for the sake of a few pounds, she would help me out if I got stuck. It's very kind of her, but it's all about standing on my own two feet again isn't it? I wouldn't have the first clue what was a priceless antique and what was worthless old junk. I suspect, looking round that there is more of the latter. I would have to be guided by what I could live with and what I could afford.

I've invested most of my meagre savings in a new bed, and bought the white goods in the kitchen from the previous owners of my new flat. I've been given some stuff too; somebody's old sofa and a television set. The last few essentials I'm hoping to get from here. The guide prices in the catalogue, which itself seemed expensive but it has got some lovely full colour photographs of the more expensive items, seem astronomical. I've been having a good poke round and there's this whole section at the back of this huge barn that's cordoned off, which contains stuff that seems to be badly soiled, broken or labelled as not working. They use a notice with AF written on it – it means As Found, so there's something wrong and the guide price reflects that. It's up to the buyer to work out what the problem is, and whether it matters.

It's what Aunty Cynth would call *The Dregs.* Out of the decent stuff I've selected two pairs of curtains, a coffee table and two bedside units, as well as a set of pans, but the only item I quite liked the look of from the dregs is a rickety old chair. I couldn't try it for comfort as it's not stable enough, but it would need doing up anyway – the fabric is worn and stained, and coming loose from the braiding where it attaches to the wood. As I stood wondering whether it was worth a punt I watched a man pick it up and front legs fell off! Oh dear.

*

I've bought a few bits, including the rickety chair. There were no bids, so I offered £5 and the auctioneer brought the hammer down that quickly. The auction's been fun. You can't actually do like they show on TV programmes, and bid for something you don't mean to, if you sneeze or accidentally put your hand up or something. If they are unsure they will ask whether you meant to bid or not. It's very tempting if you really, really like the look of something, to bid over what it's worth. I got all the stuff I'd planned to bid on. There was a lovely chair that I fancied for the living room. It went way too high, but it's given me an idea of how my sad one might look one day.

The porter who helped put the stuff in the back of my hatchback said it was a good job the chair had fallen apart, or it wouldn't all have fitted. The front legs had already parted company and the seat frame was leaning forward at a drunken angle from the frame of a shaped backrest, joined to the two rear legs. I decided to deal with the wood first. If the whole could not be made rigid again there was no point in wasting money fabric, trimming and stuffing.

It was easy to see the problem. The glue in the mortise and tenon joints had dried out completely. Scraping out all the old glue, and replacing it with fresh was enough to strengthen the wooden frame again.

The next stage was shopping. I visited the sewing shop in town and bought webbing, enough upholstery fabric to cover the seat and back of the chair, flame retardant foam filling, and braiding to hide the edges. I borrowed Aunty Cynth's heavy-duty staple gun, and watched film after film on the internet before putting on a mask and stripping off all the old torn material, braid and horsehair, and dropping them in the kitchen waste bin. It was the third handful of horsehair that gave me pause. It clunked when it hit the base of the bin and simple curiosity made me wonder why fabric or stuffing would clunk against the base of a plastic bin. I rummaged around, sending up clouds of dirt and dust until my hand closed on a small metal object. It was a ring; a woman's ring set with what looked like a generous-sized diamond.

My first thought was delight; my second was to wonder whether I really had any right to this. I had bought a broken chair for £5, then spent nearly twice as much renovating it. I looked out the contract I had signed with the saleroom, and it seemed that I had bought the item *as found*, therefore the ring was part of my purchase.

I couldn't rest easy though. I felt that I should at least try. I contacted the saleroom, who told me that they could not release information about where the chair had come from. They could tell me some bits however. The chair was part of a job lot bought in when a business had gone into liquidation. It had first been offered at a sale several months previously, then gone into what Aunty Cynth called the *Dregs,* and the auction house called the *Sin Bin*. The business owner had since died and the proceeds from the sale were simply going to pay creditors.

They advised that as I had bought the chair in good faith, and along with it the ring, that I should wear it and enjoy it. I didn't do that. It didn't feel right, but I sold it and spent the proceeds on continuing my flat refurbishment.

I think I may go back to an auction – you can get some really good bargains if you look carefully, and some even better ones if you don't.

It's a Dog's Life

Of course I thought the attention was centred around me, arrogant little sausage that I am. That's what they call me, my people, a sausage dog. How rude is that? I prefer it when people say I am fiesty, which seems more positive somehow. Not that there's anything wrong with sausages, I like a banger as much as the next pup, but to suggest that I look like one is another thing altogether. Of course my breed used to be called dachshunds, but in the mid 1950's World War II was still too recent to be comfortable. Those great big German Shepherds had the same problem and for years people pretended that they had really come from Alsace in France.

We are clever little dogs though. Do you know that when I first came to live here with my people they had the same car exactly as the family next door? Same make, same model, same colour even – a rather gloomy looking dark green – but I never once got off the chair and dashed to the door when I heard their car arrive home. The man used to get in from work at about the same time each evening as my man did, yet I never once mixed them up. I'm proud of that.

I never liked the man next door. I never bit him or anything, but he didn't like dogs and we can always tell. I did once lift my leg up on the toe of his wellington boot when he and my man were talking together at the gate. I was bored and having a snuffle round as dogs do, and he kept pushing me away with his foot. Not kicking, just pushing. Well, I had as much right to be there as he did, and showed him with a little tiddle on the front of his boot. He laughed, but he didn't mean it. A dog knows these things.

It wasn't long after this that my people got a different car. It was smaller, but there weren't many of us in the family. It was brand new and smelled weird but I soon got used to it. They'd chosen one with a special dog bed in it, just for me. It was behind the back seat and I could see through windows at both sides and look at the traffic behind. My people called it a parcel shelf, but it was a dog bed really, or a dog shelf!

As soon as one of them opened the rear door I would be in and up onto the shelf. It was a bit of an effort, my legs aren't very long, but it was worth it for the view. A couple of times they'd only opened the door for the children to get in and I had to be hauled out again much to my disgust, but usually I went with them wherever they went.

I caused quite a stir lying on that shelf. Ever such a lot of people passed would point as if a dog was something unusual. I was beginning to think it must be because I was such a handsome chap but then I heard my man explaining to someone. It seems that it was the new car that was unusual. You see until then most cars had been black or dark green, with the occasional one a dirty beige colour. This was different. It was a Hillman Minx and most of it was pale sunshine yellow, with the top part and all the roof silver grey. As I lay there being chauffeured around I never saw another that sort of colour; no wonder people looked and pointed.

I used to love going out in the car with my man driving. Going out with my woman driving was quite different. He was very smooth and careful in the car, but she, although she was very nice, was rather more erratic, and that's being polite. There were lots of sudden stops and starts. I lost count of the number of times she stopped so unexpectedly that I was flung off the shelf onto the back seat, and several times from there straight onto the floor. It doesn't half startle a pup, especially if you've just nodded off.

One breakfast morning when I must have been about six or seven my man said he would be picking up the new car after work. I wasn't bothered until one of the children asked why a new car, and he said he couldn't afford to keep the Minx any longer. I panicked then. If they were needing to downgrade from an old Minx it must be to a very small car or a very old car, or both.

It was a winter's afternoon and dark before my man came home from work, and I was waiting for him in the front window as usual. A car swung into the drive and I didn't know if it was him or not. This car was much bigger and much newer than the Minx, and it had double headlights on the front, most impressive. I couldn't understand it. It was definitely my man who got out though, so I ran to meet him with wags and licks. The child who had asked why the change of car was confused as well, until my man explained. Because the Minx was getting old it needed money spending on it, and rather than spend a lot on an old car it was more sensible to sell it and put the money towards a newer one.

That weekend we went out in the new car. The only thing I wasn't sure about was that there was no parcel shelf! For some reason the back window sloped the other way and there wasn't room for one. Perhaps they'd chosen that model because I was getting a bit old to keep getting thrown on the floor. I would just lie on the back seat between the children or on the floor at their feet. Sometimes, for a change, I would lie in the front passenger footwell and one day all these possible variations were nearly my undoing.

We'd all four of us gone out for a day trip and had a picnic lunch by a lovely river. It was a beautiful day. The children had paddled, and so had I in a really shallow bit. When it came time to go everything was packed in the car and the journey home began. I know I've grumbled about my woman's driving but I was so grateful to her for what happened next. For some reason known only to herself my woman suddenly turned round to the children in the back of the car and asked, 'who's got the dog?' and it turned out that nobody had the dog – I wasn't there. I hadn't got back into the car after the picnic stop, and nobody had checked.

My people decide that it was safer to not take

the children back with them. They were frightened that I had maybe been run over, or was stuck in the river, or had just disappeared. They left the children in a café, having had a word with the owner, and then hurried back to the site of our picnic. Where was I? I was running round and round in frantic circles exactly where the car been parked at lunchtime. Of course I only knew all this afterwards once we were all reunited and I had stopped shivering enough to listen to what they were saying.

So now I make sure that whenever one of the car doors is opened I get in. if they're not planning to take me with them they can lift me out again, but I'm not taking any more chances.

Concorde

It hadn't been planned of course; how could it be? Katie had been told at the last antenatal visit, that her estimated due date of 3rd December was way too optimistic and not to make any plans for Christmas. Of course by Christmas her baby was nearly six weeks old, but that was all in the future.

She wanted something tangible to remind her of the day, and so kept the Manchester Evening News that her husband brought into the hospital for her to read that evening.

The front page headlines were all about an unscheduled landing of the iconic *White Lady*. This was the first Concorde commercial flight to fly into Manchester Airport. Concorde G-BOAA had been diverted due to fog at London Heathrow, and had landed from the USA late the previous evening, before it could travel on to London when the fog cleared on the morning that Katie gave birth. The plane apparently was too large, and the wrong shape to be towed to a gate, and so was left waiting for clearance at the end of Pier B.

Purely by coincidence in 2003, by which time her baby was grown up with a baby of her own, Katie and her little granddaughter were out and about one morning, in search of a craft shop she had heard good things about. It dealt mainly mail order, but had a retail counter also and was only a few miles from Katie's home in the village of Mobberley, which is directly under the flight path for Manchester Airport's second runway, the longer runway of the two, at three thousand, two hundred metres.

The lanes around the tiny village of Mobberley were crammed with cars. All the verges were blocked where drivers, mainly men, had parked up, and there was much evidence of binoculars and cameras, all pointing hopefully in the same direction. A police officer was doing his best to keep traffic moving, and when Katie was eventually able to creep her car forward and reach him she asked what was going on.

'It's Concorde due in shortly,' he told her, 'Last commercial flight into Manchester before being decommissioned.' The date was 22nd October 2003.

That same Concorde was given pride of place at Manchester the following week. Tickets were sold to a gala dinner event, with the tables set and the meal served under the shelter of Concorde's massive wings, for the not insignificant sum of £90 a ticket. After the dinner *The White Lady,* or as she was sometimes called, *The Time Machine,* was put on display at the Runway Visitor Park. This second nickname had been given to her because, given local time differences, she was the only plane that could theoretically land before she had taken off. She is still on display there, although these days she is kept under cover.

Purely by chance Katie then came across another connection with Concorde. The Fairey Delta 2 was a prominent research aircraft developed in the 1950s. Its predecessor, the Fairey Delta 1 had first been considered in 1947, at which time Katie's own mother worked for Fairey Engineering, based out of Manchester Airport, which in those days was called Ringway Airport. Katie's mother had left school aged fourteen, and worked for Fairey Engineering throughout the war, and until she married.
 Many of the ideas tried on the FD1 aircraft were discarded for various reasons, but successes included the droop-nose concept, and the delta wing configuration. These were refined into the FD2. This plane in its turn, served as an experimental platform for high-speed flight, and paved the way for the British Aircraft Corporation (BAC) 221, a critical link in the development of the iconic Concorde.

The BAC221 included the now universally recognisable droop nose. At supersonic speeds the FD2 was flown with the nose in the neutral position, but for take-off and landing the nose could be lowered to give the pilot a better field of vision. All these developments came together to inform the capability of Concorde.

Many years later the family had chance to visit the Concorde that was parked up at Yeovilton and

Katie marvelled that this wonder of engineering, capable of such amazing feats of speed, was such a long, thin tube. She felt quite claustrophobic, and was glad to get out and admire it from outside.

It seemed her to be fitting that her family had been in on the start of Concorde; tangentially around for its inaugural local journey, and was again there at the end.

The Electric Chair

Disaster struck on a Tuesday afternoon, which was unfortunate to put it mildly. If it had happened in the morning my cleaning lady Phyllis would have been able to help, although she's tiny – have you heard the expression *seven stone wet through*? Well that describes Phyllis perfectly. Anyway, she'd already left and wouldn't be back till the following Tuesday morning. If it had happened the next day it wouldn't have been too bad, because my nephew usually calls round on a Wednesday, and would either have been here or been on his way and could have helped me.

Now, I'm a well-built girl, as my late father used to say, though that was a long time ago. I'm over eighty now, still well-built, or rather big-boned and I make no apology for enjoying my food. There is little else to look forward to at my age. I get my lunches delivered, you know those companies that make it all for you, so you just have to pop it in the oven, or even the microwave. Except I find that there's never really sufficient food for my appetite, and I usually supplement it with a few boiled potatoes, or some bread, or even a few chips.

The puddings are lovely, but then again, they are very stingy with the quantities. I find some evaporated milk or tinned custard poured over, or a scoop of ice-cream, or even a slice or two of cake helps to fill the gap.

Of course they only provide the main meals – lunch and dinner. For breakfast I have fruit, usually on top of a couple of Weetabix, and then a slice or two of toast with jam. Then for supper, because I can't ever seem to sleep well on an empty stomach, I have cheese and biscuits, or maybe a few sweet biscuits; just to line my stomach for sleep. I like a milky drink too at bedtime: hot chocolate or Ovaltine sits nicely I find.

I had to have a hip replacement operation a couple of years ago, which is when I started employing Phyllis. She's a lovely young lady – well, I say young, she's a lot younger and more agile than me. I got this chair then too. The electric chair, that's what my nephew calls it; not very nice is it? The correct word is orthopaedic. They're quite expensive, but you can adjust the sitting position and there's a footrest, which really helps the hip. I find that there's lots of support across my back too. The back of the chair itself is made of three separate squabs that can be lifted and a rolled-up towel or similar pushed underneath, so that you can be sure to find a position where you are comfortable. I sound like an advert don't I? But they really are impressive. There are times when I've been sitting here in the evening and I'm so comfortable that it's a real effort to get up and get ready for bed. The best bit about this chair for me is that the whole seat will tip right forward at the touch of a button and virtually stand you upright. Now that really is a boon for the hip! They make them in all different sizes too, and you can try them in the shop to see which is best for you before you buy.

Which is all very well, and I love the chair as you can tell. One thing they don't tell you about in their blurb though, is that there is a risk during a power cut, of the chair being stuck in one position. And that is where we are now – or at least, that is where I am now! Stuck!

I had put the television on as I usually do in the evenings, and settled myself comfortably here in my magic chair, and the power went off. The television I can live without. In fact I'm quite happy to sit here in the dark and just go to sleep, but I will be needing the bathroom before too long and that's a bit of a worry. Fruitlessly I keep pressing the button, but of course the lights and television would come back on if everything was back to normal, so I know it's a waste of time. It's just instinctive.

I'm beginning to get a bit peckish now. Fortunately my mantel clock doesn't run off electricity and so I know I must have dozed for a bit. I did wonder if I could get out of the chair unaided, but with the footrest up I don't think I can.

I've struggled to twist round and tried to lever myself out with the help of the chair arm and my stick, which is never far away, but with my hip I can only go one way, and that's towards the wall, and there isn't enough space. I've been able to reach the rug that lies on the sofa and drag that across my legs, which is a comfort. The central heating hasn't cut in, and it's getting cold. In doing so, I'm afraid I caught the edge of the table lamp and knocked it on the floor, which is another problem that will need sorting out.

Phew! We are back in business. The television came back on, although the lamp seems to be beyond help. The buttons are working too on my magic chair. I never thought such a small thing would make me so happy. I've been to the loo, so I'm comfortable now. I'll go and get myself some supper in a minute when my heart rate's back to normal. I think I'll eat it sitting at the kitchen table though, in case it happens again.

I know now that I can cope with a power cut. I'll start keeping a torch and the rug closer at hand, just in case of problems in the future. I'll also keep some food in the little pocket that helpfully provided on the side of the chair – a bar of chocolate maybe. That would be good. I'll ask Phyllis to get me organised next time she comes.

The Lavender Bed

Henry was his name, and he had moved into this little house seven years ago. A keen gardener, he had kept himself busy digging, planting and weeding. Even on wet, miserable days he would use the time to pore over seed catalogues, tidy the greenhouse and hunt through his gardening magazines making plans for changes for next year.

There was something so optimistic about gardening he thought. Even if the season was disastrous, experiments failed and well-loved, apparently healthy plants died, there was always next season to look forward to, and new things to try.

The first two years after he moved he had attended many flower shows, gleaning ideas, rejecting ideas and generally enjoying himself. He particularly loved the last hour or so of the last day of these shows, when the exhibits were sold off at bargain prices.

His gardens, front and rear, were small. The back was largely laid to a patio, and he had invested in raised beds around the perimeter. He knew a time would come when bending down would be beyond him, and this way he could keep his hobby alive.

It was a social activity too, especially when he was working in the front garden, weeding, trimming the mixed hedges and topping up the birdbath. In hot weather he kept a dog bowl, regularly topped-up, by the gate. So many people seemed to walk their dogs in the heat of the day, and he felt sorry for them. A little drink must surely make them more comfortable and help them enjoy their walks more. In his younger days Henry had always had a dog, but these days the walking would be too much for him, so he just enjoyed being able to bring a little happiness to other people's dogs. Often the dog-walkers would stop and chat about how he was and what he was doing. It passed the time.

Three years after he moved in, he redesigned the front garden. He had seen a horrendous article in the newspaper about the potential demise of bees. At one time Henry had kept bees, belonging to a club that met in a bespoke area of a local park. He would have loved to keep bees in his garden, but the houses here were so close to each other, that it really wasn't a practical proposition. He had to think of the neighbours.

The garden was largely laid to gravel, but there was an L-shaped flower bed along the drive and under the windows. This he filled with lavender because he loved the scent and it was very attractive to the bees. He bought the two most frequently occurring varieties in the catalogue, Hidcote and Munstead. He reckoned that if any of the plants failed to thrive he would easily be able to replace the odd one at relatively little expense.

The plants he ordered arrived in three-inch pots. He chastised himself, knowing that these days he should be thinking in metric units, but he was too old to change now, and three-inch pots they would always be.

Having unpacked and watered them carefully, he turned his attention to where they would be put. Lavender plants dislike wet, heavy soil such as the clay in Henry's L-shaped flower beds. He set about gradually digging out some of the top soil, and moving it, with the help of a friend, to top up the raised beds at the back. Then he added copious amounts of grit, more than he would ever have thought possible. It was a big job, and by the time it was finished it was time to plant out the lavender.

It looked a little puny the first year and a couple of plants didn't make it through the winter. Henry planted the two varieties alternately and was pleased with the result. It was the following year that next door's gardener, a lovely helpful man, suggested that he took some cuttings before too long. Apparently, which Henry didn't know, lavender plants tend to get woody and unattractive after three or four years, and the appearance of his garden would benefit from them being replaced. It would have to wait. Henry was not prepared to get in amongst the plants at that point, swarming as they were with busy bees. So the following year he would take cuttings between June and September, as advised by his mentor.

This year though, Henry is indisposed. His health has taken a nose-dive and he is confined to the house, where he frets about the state of his garden. Next door's gardener offered to help him out, but he doesn't have the funds to pay a gardener, so had to decline. Even so, he opened the curtains one morning to find the gardener cutting his hedge. When Henry challenged him, he was told that as next door's was being done anyway, another few metres of hedge made little difference. There would be no charge.

Henry knew that this was an act of pure kindness. It wasn't just whizzing along the top of the hedge with the electric hedgecutter, it was sweeping up all the clippings, putting them in the garden waste bin, and then moving the bin to the gate, something else Henry struggled with. He noticed too that the ailing lavender plants had been consigned to the recycling bin and replacements had been added. He wondered whether there were any people in the world kinder than gardeners.

As Henry's health began to improve he took more interest again in his garden. Perhaps by September he would feel well enough to take more lavender cuttings. But as he sat there for so long each day, looking out at the front garden, he realised something. Once again the bees were making the most of the nectar.

Henry liked to think that now the bees had found this rich source of thirty lavender plants that seemed to be thriving in his front garden, they would continue to visit for many years.

A Tale of Two Nurses

That year the anniversary seemed to affect her more than it had in previous years. Of course it was a special anniversary; perhaps that was the reason.

It was a time that had passed for Amelia in a blur. Gran had fallen in the middle of the previous year, and at almost ninety years old, obviously the signs weren't good. Added to that, Amelia's mother had been diagnosed with cancer nearly eighteen months previously, and was now in a specialist oncologist unit attached to a different hospital on the other side of the city. Amelia visited her mum every day, and knew that she would not be coming home.

When Amelia arrived at the hospital that fateful Monday morning, her mother was clearly struggling. Amelia found the young nurse, Johnny, who was allocated as the lead on her mum's care and asked that she be given additional pain killers as she was in some distress. He checked the chart and told

Amelia that it would be another two hours before more morphine could be administered.

'There must be something you can do,' Amelia begged, 'it's inhuman watching her suffering like this. I don't want this to be my last memory of her.'

Johnny seemed to consider her words for a moment, then: 'Just a minute,' he disappeared behind the nurses' station and joined Amelia a few minutes later with a white cloth over a kidney dish in one hand. 'Amelia, could you leave me alone with your mum for a few moments please?'

Amelia took the opportunity to nip to the loo and when she returned Johnny was once again at the nurses' station and there was no sign of the kidney dish. Entering her mum's room Amelia could immediately see that she was much calmer. Whereas she had been distressed and heavily perspiring, now she lay peacefully, her breathing calm and regular. She was even smiling. She passed away forty minutes later.

Apart from all the practical issues to be dealt with there was also Amelia's Gran to be told, and she was very grateful that her aunt and uncle took that step rather than her. The following day she went to visit her Gran. The old lady knew that the death of her daughter had been expected. Just the previous week she had said to Amelia, 'Your mum's not going to be coming home from hospital is she? I ask you because I know you will tell me the truth, not just tell me what I want to hear.'

Amelia had agreed that she thought it unlikely. Now, with her daughter gone, the old lady's thoughts turned understandably to her own future. 'I won't have anywhere to live now, will I?'

'Of course you will, Gran,' Amelia tried to reassure, 'We've talked about this and we will make changes to our house, so you can have a downstairs bedroom, and we'll put a loo under the stairs like at Mum's.'

Did the old lady believe it? Who knows? Certainly Amelia knew it was most unlikely to happen.

The following day a trip to the undertaker confirmed her mother's funeral for the following Monday, and it occurred to Amelia that with all the family and friends wanting to pay their respects, and the local minister carrying out the service, Gran would potentially be on her own.

She phoned Gran's ward and the phone was answered by the Ward Sister. Amelia explained that her mother's funeral would be on Monday afternoon; this was Gran's daughter's funeral, and she wondered whether there was a hospital chaplain or someone who could sit with the old lady, just so she wasn't on her own at that time.

The sister's response was brutal. Afterwards Amelia wondered whether she should have reported such crass insensitivity, but stunned as she was at the time, she did nothing.

'Oh, I don't think you need worry about Gran on Monday,' the sister told her, 'We're not expecting your grandmother to make it through the weekend! She's going downhill very quickly.' Amelia was so shocked at the way she was given this news that she just put the phone down.

The brutal sister was quite correct. Amelia's

Gran died on the Friday morning, and the round of visits to undertakers, caterers and other officialdom had to be repeated. Again Amelia was so grateful to other members of the family, who seemed to totally understand how overwhelming it all was, and took on those responsibilities. She was especially appreciative of her uncle's input, as he took on the lion's share, mindful that his wife had just lost both her mother and her only sister.

It seemed to pass in a blur, with occasional jolts of reality; finding her mother's flowers still on display at the crematorium when they arrived for her Gran's service four days later; family members – some really close – who were not permitted to take two compassionate leave days off work in the same week, and so had to choose which funeral to attend.

Looking back, one thing that particularly stuck in Amelia's mind was the contrast between the attitude of the two nurses; Johnny who was so compassionate, even though she suspected that in administering that final drug to her mother he may have ended her life. It was the humane thing to do. The other was the brutal sister, who may just have been having a bad day, but who was so insensitive to Amelia's feelings as to blurt out that she expected her Grandmother's imminent death.

Amelia hoped that, were she to find herself *in extremis* it would be a nurse like Johnny who took responsibility for her.

The Bumps

Four years ago. It was December. Daz's wife was drawing the curtains by 4 o'clock to keep in what warmth there was. There was a crisp frost glistening across the road and even lower temperatures were threatened overnight. He had checked that his car doors were locked earlier. With a single width driveway he necessarily had to leave the car on the road at the front of the property in order for his wife to get hers out. It always seemed to be congested out there. The people directly opposite had parking for two cars, but with two adults and two grown-up children, each with a boyfriend there could at any time be as many as six cars outside their house alone.

Daz and his wife were in the kitchen when the doorbell rang. Insulated behind the noise of the television they had heard no indication of anything wrong, and she was surprised to open the door to find their neighbour from the house opposite, who was visibly upset.

'I'm so sorry, I'm dashing out in a hurry and

I've reversed into your car. I need to get my daughter Paige down to the hospital and my mind wasn't on what I was doing. I'm so sorry.' He was visibly shaken.

Daz had heard him and came to stand behind his wife at the door, 'Don't worry,' he said, hoping to offer comfort. 'Cars can be fixed. Your daughter's more important. Go and take her to the hospital, do what you need to do. Drive carefully and we'll sort everything out in the daylight tomorrow.'

After he and his daughter had driven off, Daz put on a coat and, using his phone as a torch, went to inspect the damage. He was unconcerned, 'It's not much,' he said shrugging out of the coat, 'He's caught the rear door just behind the driver's door, that's all. I'll pop it up to the garage when they can fit it in, and they'll sort it. We probably won't even put it through the insurance. Our neighbour has enough problems without losing his no claims discount.'

In the daylight however, and talking to the man at the garage it became obvious that the problem was more significant. The impact had taken place between the driver's door and the rear door, exactly on the strengthening pillar that passed from the chassis on one side, across the roof and down to join the chassis on the other. This pillar had been hit, not hard but it had been bent and that was an issue in terms of the future safety of the car. The man at the garage explained that he could not repair it, as its integrity was compromised, that the insurance company would say the same, as would any other repair shop he took the car to. So the car was a write-off.

This was a blow, a severe blow, but a replacement car was eventually bought, the insurance company of the man across the road paid out, and everyone was, reasonably, happy.

Fast forward to three weeks ago. It was a Thursday evening. In the morning Daz's wife had gone into town to have coffee with a friend and, because he had a regular meeting to attend that evening, Daz left his car on the road at the front of their house, the first time he had done this since the accident.

At ten to seven, just before Daz was due to leave, the doorbell rang. His wife answered the door to the same man, who said, 'I'm so sorry, I'm afraid I've done it again.'

This time the damage was superficial. The impact hit the driver's door, and was a fairly cosmetic procedure to put right. It beggars belief though, how someone can reverse into a car parked under a lit street light, then four years later, do the exact same thing again.

Daz and his wife don't leave either car on the front any more. They have a system now of swapping over the cars and always bringing one into the drive if the other one has gone out. It's inconvenient but, as Daz says, a lot less inconvenient than having to get the car repaired . . . yet again!

I Wish I'd looked after me Teeth

Have you read that poem by Pam Ayres? I was reminded of it today when I thought of Ralph and his difficulties. Ralph was not a well-to-do man, in fact he was what is referred to as a Traveller, as was his wife; not a Romany or from any of the noted travelling communities, but someone who found it difficult to settle in one place. They lived modestly, and Ralph's only real extravagance was the copious amount of sugar he put in his tea, and the toffees to which he seemed addicted. He and his young wife would go wherever there was work; picking fruit, gardening, clearing gutters – you name it, Ralph would have a go at it. His wife was a cleaner, laundress, unofficial childminder, and would pick up work wherever she could.

Ralph seldom attended a dentist. He had suffered a bad experience as a young teenager, and that was enough for him. What happened was that his mother took a fancy to, and put a lot of faith in, this dentist near to where they were staying when she visited him with a problem of her own. He was a charlatan. He refused to countenance conventional anaesthesia, which in those days was pretty basic, and instead claimed to be able to hypnotise his patients.

Perhaps Ralph's mother was particularly susceptible to his charms, but she came home having been relieved of a painful molar, singing his praises and insisting that young Ralph visit him. She parroted his rhetoric that hypnosis was much safer than drugs, and drugs had to be paid for in those days before the National Health Service, so he could save them money too. Ralph was fifteen years old and had been having trouble with what they suspected was emerging wisdom teeth for some time. He was in a good deal of discomfort and agreed. Granted the dentist had a very soothing voice but Ralph found himself totally unmoved by his attempts at relaxation, in this way. Certainly he would have much preferred conventional pain relief, although this would have been either ether, or nitrous oxide, known as *laughing gas*.

Young Ralph was not laughing as he left the surgery, his face swollen and sore. He was unable to eat anything more substantial than soup for days, and he swore never to go near a dentist again. But then things changed. He married and a child was expected to the couple, and subsequently a daughter was born. This change in circumstances coincided with a philanthropic period and Ralph and his family found that they were eligible for a modest council house. For the first time in their lives they stayed in one place.

Ralph was employed at a local factory, and his wife continued her domestic cleaning. As the child would need to attend school in the future, they agreed that this stability was needed in their lives.

Kezia was a bright girl, the apple of her father's eye. Ralph's wife determined that she would have regular access to a dentist, and registered them all with a Polish man who had a well-established practice in the nearest town. Ralph refused to go.

The years passed. Kezia left school and became a civil servant. In due course she met a young man, whom Ralph found very intimidating. This now elderly man, who could only read slowly and haltingly, had a prospective son-in-law who was a university graduate and who now worked in the city, although Ralph had no idea what that meant. The young couple were getting married. With a lot of help from the groom's family they were able to put a deposit on a house, and a wedding date was set.

Over the years Ralph's teeth had deteriorated considerably. He had eventually accepted that he would be reduced to a diet of pap and soup, or have them all out and replaced with dentures. He remembered that his own father had had all his teeth removed as a twenty-first birthday present; not an unusual occurrence at the time, but things move on. By the time Ralph accepted that he needed help, replacing teeth with dentures was a last resort.

The long awaited wedding day arrived and after the ceremony the key players took their designated places at the top table. Ralph was very nervous – he would have to make a speech and, not a natural orator, he had been practising and practising, whilst his wife and daughter had been organising the service and the wedding breakfast.

The table setting was beautiful, with thick white damask tablecloths and napkins, the cake on a side table to be cut later. The meal was superb, although Ralph found the array of cutlery as confusing as he did the choice of wines. His new son-in-law helpfully led by example and Ralph's embarrassment was averted. He gamely worked his way through more courses than he had ever before encountered, relieved that the bill for all this largesse had not fallen on his shoulders.

Nerves drove him to the bathroom before making his speech and the waiters began to clear tables. In a lull of expectation, as often happens at such events, a sudden shout went up from the top table. The young waitress, not yet out of her teens, had picked up Ralph's discarded napkin and found nestling inside his set of false teeth, which she then dropped in alarm.

Awkward laughter greeted Ralph's return to the dining room, and he returned to the top table to find his napkin and his teeth had gone. The waitress returned almost immediately with the teeth in a glass bowl. She apologised for having inadvertently dropped them, and told him that they had been washed, after having fallen to the floor. Ralph stumbled through his speech, and in the privacy of his room later explained to his wife what had happened.

One of the courses was such that his dentures couldn't cope with it. He had slipped them out, so that he could continue eating, in the vain hope that he would not draw attention to himself. His embarrassment was excruciating as he thought back over the laughter that had accompanied his return to the top table.

'Eeh lass,' he said to his wife, 'It were a reet good do, but I wish I'd looked after me teeth.'

Toffee's Tale

The arrival of Toffee had been something of a surprise. It is always pleasant to receive a gift, especially a gift from her daughter Jodie, but Toffee was a puppy, a tiny, fluffy, incontinent puppy.

Lynn lived alone in a first floor flat, which brought its own complications. She had a few health problems, nothing she couldn't cope with, but being unable to work there was not a lot of money around. She was concerned because keeping a pet can prove expensive, but Jodie promised to help and Lynn couldn't deny that when she looked into Toffee's funny, smiling little face, it made her happy.

But then her health suffered a further blow. She succumbed to a rare disorder in which the body's immune system attacks the nerves. Weakness and tingling in the hands and feet are usually the first symptoms. These sensations can quickly spread, eventually paralysing the whole body.

The precursor to the paralysis in Lynn's case was a string of bad infections, and this seems to be common amongst sufferers. With her other health complications, Lynn was hospitalised for months. But this is Toffee's story.

Jodie did all that she could to help. She took the little dog to stay with her but, having a young family of her own, she was already missing her mother's support in that Lynn had collected her children from school and stayed with them several times a week. Eventually she had to admit defeat, but managed to find a friend who offered to take Toffee until Lynn recovered.

This friend, incredibly kind and well-meaning as she was, did not have the time to give Toffee the attention a young dog needed, and before long Toffee was becoming a liability. He was also unsure about his new toilet regime and began to mess in the house. Eventually Jodie's friend had to admit defeat, and reluctantly the decision was made that Toffee would have to be rehomed. Lynn was still in hospital, and even when discharged, she would not be able to cope with getting the dog downstairs from her flat and outside when he needed to go out. She also would not be able to exercise him adequately.

Toffee was rehomed with a family Stoke on Trent, where Lynn's cousin lived and where there are many lovely country walks ideal for a young energetic dog. He was passed on to a family who already had a rescue dog Lilly, and who had the funds to deal with whatever needs may arise in Toffee's future. Lilly was a sociable little girl who showed no jealousy to the incomer.

Lynn's cousin was also a dog owner. One morning while out walking her own dog she met a woman with two dogs coming towards her. This cousin had only met Toffee once, as a very young puppy, and had the woman not referred to him by name, she would not have recognised the adult dog. When asked the name of her dogs the woman told her they were Lilly and Toffee, and that both had been rehomed to her care, Toffee quite recently. Lynn's cousin was delighted to see Toffee looking so alert, happy and well-groomed. They chatted for a few minutes before she revealed that she knew who Toffee was, and where he had come from. Toffee's new owner said that he was a delight, and had obviously been very well cared for when he was younger. She said that a few days' intensive work on his toileting and other routines and Toffee had settled in very quickly.

Lynn's cousin took a photograph of her dog playing with Lilly and Toffee, and asked permission to show it to her cousin. She didn't want to show it to Lynn for a while, worried that it may be upsetting. When eventually she did see it, she said she was delighted to see Toffee looking so well and happy.

It had been a long recovery process, with Lynn unable to live independently for over six months. Letting Toffee go to a new home, difficult though that was, had definitely been the right thing to do.

Nine Patterned Shirts

Another Friday, another pile of ironing.

It just wasn't possible. She ironed every week without fail, the chore she hated the most, and once again there were nine patterned shirts. Nine! Once again, as most weeks, she marvelled at a man who could wear more clothes than there were days in the week. They weren't easy to iron either. He eschewed short sleeves, opting in hot weather to fold up the button cuffs of the long sleeves. They all had what he called button-down collars too, with at least two, and sometimes three tiny buttons as a feature around the neck, the third being at the centre back, a little vanity feature, if you will. In order to iron them properly she had to undo all these every time. He never did, and never seemed to appreciate the struggle for her arthritic fingers every single week.

The fabric he selected never seemed to be the easy-iron stuff that she chose for her own clothes, and it took Faye an inordinately long time to smooth out all the creases. Most were checked, or striped and she struggled with the stripes on several of them. There was probably a name for the condition where someone couldn't look at narrow striped fabrics without the world spinning, and a feeling of dizziness. Every week, hunched over the ironing board, she intended to look it up, but every week she forgot once the detested chore was completed.

Between them she and Lewis had brought up a family of three sons. As soon as the boys were old enough, Faye had shown them how to iron their clothes, and told them it was their responsibility. They must iron their school shirts, but they could choose whether to bother with their casual clothes. She would not be doing it. They took it in good part, developing a routine where they would take turns, so each ironed once every three weeks. She said nothing about how often they should change their shirts, their peers would let them know if there was a problem. She made sure there was plenty of deodorant available and she also pointed out that thoroughly washing their necks would keep their shirts looking fresh for longer. They had, one by one, grown and flown the nest, leaving Faye with just her husband's shirts to iron.

Looking over the ironing board now, she stared at the laundry pile; four handkerchiefs and the inevitable nine shirts. Her own clothes had been washed along with his, then hung straight on hangers and were now back in her wardrobe. Hey-ho, she tested the steam on the iron, and began.

If it was just Faye's clothes to be laundered, she could dispense altogether with the cumbersome ironing board, just smoothing anything that was desperately creased on a clean towel spread on the kitchen worktop, but now she found herself working through this multi-coloured pile of fabric. Of course she really knew why there would be nine shirts. Lewis insisted on a clean one every day. Fair enough, but he also wanted a clean one if he went out in the evenings, which he routinely did twice a week. On Tuesdays he would go down to the club to play darts with the boys. Faye failed to believe that these boys would care, nor even notice, whether Lewis was wearing a clean shirt, but he insisted. Then on Friday nights, like tonight, they would often go out together; to the cinema, or for a meal, or occasionally to the theatre in town. She got cleaned up and changed before doing that, of course, and so did Lewis, which led to yet another shirt to be ironed the following Friday morning. She always saved ironing the handkerchiefs until the shirts were all done, getting the awkward part of the job out of the way first. With a sigh, she stopped daydreaming and spread the first shirt across the board, ready to begin.

* * *

Another Friday morning, the weeks just fly by. Only eight shirts to be ironed today, and somehow the chore didn't seem too bad. It had been quite a week. Lewis had gone as usual to the club last Tuesday week, wearing a fresh shirt as always. Tonight though he wouldn't be needing a clean shirt; he wouldn't be going out. As usual, she counted the shirts as she completed them, and for a split second she forgot and was puzzled when she got to eight and only the handkerchiefs remained. Just for a moment though. Of course Lewis was already wearing his best shirt. The shirt with the stripes, which she had ironed for the last time last Friday.

She carefully emptied the water reservoir and unplugged the iron, then took the laundry through to the bedroom, where she laid it all out on the bed. She folded all the shirts, and all those remaining in the wardrobe, and stowed them in two supermarket carriers. *Bag for Life* they announced cheerfully, which she thought ironic. She would ask her neighbour to take them along to the charity shop sometime next week, along with the hated ironing board. Everybody had been so kind, offering to assist Faye in any way they could. The neighbour would feel that she had done her bit to help. It was a shame about Lewis's best shirt, the red striped one, but at least this way no one else would have to suffer ironing those dizzying stripes. It was currently being worn just one last time by Lewis, and then would be condemned to the flames of the crematorium tomorrow afternoon.

Heart of Gold

Richie has a heart of gold. A lot of people have said so. He is one of those people who would volunteer to help anyone out if they needed it. The problem is that Richie's help generally turned a molehill into a mountain; a problem into a disaster. His skills and judgement just don't live up to his good intentions.

From his kitchen window one morning he spotted that it was starting to rain. His neighbour had two lines full of washing hanging in the garden. Richie ran round and banged on the door to let his neighbour know, but there was no reply. Dashing around to the back, he grabbed the armfuls of washing, and the peg bag and headed towards his own back door. Suddenly the neighbour appeared at her own back door, 'Richie, what are you doing? I've just hung all that out.'

'It's raining,' said Richie, only then noticing

that the rain had been short-lived, amounting to nothing more than a few spits and spots, and that now the sun was shining again.

'Well it was . . . I thought . . .'

His neighbour gave an audible sigh, 'Thought you were helping, yes I know. Hand it over.' Richie went to hand the armfuls over the low fence, mindful of not standing in the flowerbed, and in doing so he dropped a nappy, a white sock and a jumper onto the muddy ground. 'Sorry.' He lifted the load higher, snagging a pair of tights on the rough wood of the fence as he did so.

'Thanks.' His neighbour was abrupt, taking the load in through her back door and slamming it behind her.

'I was just trying to . . . help,' said Richie to the closed door.

He offered to walk the dog that lived two doors down. He knew that the husband was in hospital, and his wife seemed to be very stressed. She was grateful for the offer of help and explained where they usually walked the dog each morning. It was a big dog, strong-looking and wearing a head harness, when the neighbour brought it to the door. She handed over treats and poo bags and Richie set off for the field. He felt sorry for the dog; the head harness didn't look comfortable. Surely the dog would be happier with the lead just hooked to his collar, and he, Richie was strong enough to hold it. As he leaned down and unclipped the lead the dog spotted a squirrel and shot after it. It was over half an hour before he tired and Richie was able to lure him back using the treats. On the way the dog had rubbed the head harness down over his nose. No longer held fast by the tension of the lead, it had slid off his face and try as he might Richie couldn't find it in the grass. He returned the dog to his concerned owner and apologised. The woman couldn't understand how the head harness came to be missing.

'I'll buy you a new one,' Richie offered.

'Don't bother,' said the woman through clenched teeth, 'I need it for tonight. He's too strong for me to walk without it. I'll have to call at the pet shop on my way home from the hospital.' Another door was slammed in Richie's face.

He worried about the very elderly lady who lived opposite. He was very worried about her one morning when her burglar alarm seemed to be blaring before seven o'clock. Richie went across but nobody heard his knock on the door. He pondered what to do. Surely she must be able to hear that row; he was quite hard of hearing himself, but it was deafening – why hadn't she turned it off. All sorts of unpleasant possibilities passed through his head. Then he remembered that the woman had a nephew and his family living in the next street; perhaps they had a key. He dressed hurriedly and went round. His knocking on the door set off the next door dog barking, and he could hear water running. After a few minutes the door cracked open a few inches and the lady of the house peered out. She was dripping wet footprints along the hall, draped in a towel with another round her head.

'Sorry, I was in the shower, and my husband's in bed – he's just in from nights, and the blasted dog barking has woken him. What can I do for you?'

'It's your aunty,' Richie blurted out, 'the alarm's going and I can't make her hear. I wondered if you had a key.'

The woman sighed, 'I'll be round in a minute; I'll just get some clothes on.' The door was firmly closed.

As Richie made his way home he noticed that other alarms seemed to be going off too. Still, better safe than sorry.

The woman and her dishevelled-looking husband turned up a few minutes later. Before using their key the man banged on the door, which was opened by his aunt. 'What are you doing here so early?' she asked, 'the electric's tripped and the alarm went off. There was someone banging on the door earlier, but by the time I got there they'd gone. Hello Richie, what's the matter?'

Explanations made, the disgruntled pair made their way home, the man glaring at Richie as he passed. He realised that he'd been too hasty, and to make up for it he put the old lady's rubbish bin out the following evening when he'd done his own. Unfortunately he tripped over the kerb, and her rubbish went spilling over the footpath and the road. She found him a yard brush when he offered to clean it up, but the brush head came detached from the handle when he tried to scrub up a stubborn spillage and he had to give it back to her in two pieces. 'Okay Richie,' she said, 'I know you were only trying to help, but I'll manage it myself.'

A couple of mornings ago Richie had been crossing the small area outside the charity shop where he had recently started volunteering. A woman with a small child in a buggy was trying to offload stuff for the shop from her car. It was a bit of a struggle and Richie leapt forward to help. 'I'll get the door,' he said, meaning the shop door. She must have thought he meant the car door, which swung wide open as she let go of it, hitting the back panel of the car parked next to it. Instead of dealing with all this, the woman shoved the child back in her car, jumped in and drove away. She lowered the window and shouted sarcastically, 'Thanks for your help, not! My husband is going to be livid.' at Richie.

Then yesterday Mrs Hargreaves, who managed the shop, had given him the sack. Politely of course; he'd been volunteering on a trial basis for two weeks, and she said that they wouldn't be requiring his services after today and thanked him for his help over the past weeks. He'd seen it coming. Just yesterday morning a customer had brought a jacket over to the cash desk, complaining that there wasn't a price ticket on it. Mrs Hargreaves was working in the back of the shop and rather than disturb her Richie decided that he could show some initiative and deal with it himself.

This lady obviously didn't have much money, and he was inclined to just think of a number to let the woman get on her way, when a shout went up that brought Mrs Hargreaves scurrying through from the area where she had been sorting bags that had been left on the porch overnight.

A woman was looking frantically round the

shop, 'Where's my jacket? Hey! That's mine. I only threw it over the rail while I tried this one on.' The indignant owner glared at Richie, who had been folding it ready to put in a bag for the other customer. The price he had suggested was ridiculously low, and now both women were angry and the whole situation had to be smoothed over by Mrs Hargreaves before they each left the shop without him making a sale.

That was the last straw according to Mrs Hargreaves. Just before lunch she left Richie in the shop while she popped a few doors away to the bank on the roundabout. While she was gone a lady brought in some bedding plants. They weren't in plant pots and Richie thought they wouldn't last long bare-rooted like that. He found a cat litter tray in the back, yet to be put out for sale, so he went and dug up some soil from the patch outside the shop's back door, then he planted up the bedding as best he could, and the lady who had brought them in filled a watering can off the display, and watered them.

They had just finished, when Mrs Hargreaves returned, 'Sorry I was so long Richie,' she said, 'there was such a kerfuffle outside the bank. Someone has stripped a load of bedding plants the council planted out on the roundabout last week. Who would do that?'

She stopped and looked aghast at the plants, litter tray and soil in the shop, as a police officer came through the door. 'Well, well, well.' He glared at the donor of the stolen plants, 'I'll come to you in a minute - first of all let's have a word with this gentleman.' He indicated that Richie should go with him into the back room. Behind him another figure had also entered the shop. It was the woman whose jacket he had nearly sold.

'That's him, that's the man who tried to steal my jacket and sell it to someone else.'

Mrs Hargreaves said doubtfully, 'Officer, this is Richie's last day at the shop today. I don't think he had any intention of causing these problems, Officer. It's just a misunderstanding.'

It was all smoothed over but Mrs Hargreaves said that she wouldn't be needing him anymore, and so this morning he had been at a loose end. He grabbed a shopping bag and took the car down to the Co-op for a bottle of milk. He didn't really need milk until tomorrow, but it would give him something to do, and he might find someone to chat with.

It was as he parked up that he saw the lady. She lived a couple of roads away, and was glaring around the car park, evidently in some distress.

'Can I help you? You look worried,' Richie put his hand on her arm, and she clung to him.

'Oh yes, could you give me a lift? My husband left me here and I need to get down to the square in town as quickly as possible. Do you know it, the square in town, where the garages are?'

'Of course I do,' Richie was opening his passenger door, 'the one where all the car dealerships are.'

'That's it. That's it.' She allowed him to help with her seatbelt.

'Is your husband meeting you there?' Richie struggled to make conversation, as she emptied a purse onto her knee. It contained only a five pound note, a few coins and a Co-op loyalty card.

'He's in the shop. It'll be a surprise.'

'The Co-op?' Richie was beginning to feel uneasy, 'should you not have waited for him there?'

'Oh no, no, no. He has a car. I need the car for me.'

'You're collecting a new car! How exciting.'

'Buying a car, yes, a yellow one.'

'Lovely.' They were approaching the square now, 'which dealership have you bought it from?'

Her nose was pressed to window as Richie slowly drove past one showroom, then another. The driver behind expressed his impatience by leaning on his horn.

'That one,' she said suddenly, 'that looks a nice one, that yellow car.'

Richie was beginning to feel out of his depth, 'Yes, it looks lovely, is that the one you've bought?' he asked her, parking up on the forecourt and opening the passenger door.

'Not yet,' she said, 'but it's a nice colour. I think I'll have that one.'

A salesman came out to meet them, 'Mrs Cooper, you know you've been told not to do this. I'll have to phone your husband, and I warned you that this time the police would be involved. You damaged the door on that Prius the other day, trying to break into it with your kitchen knife.' He glared at Richie before indicating to a colleague to make a couple of phone calls.

It took only ten minutes for Mr Cooper to arrive, looking very hot and bothered, 'I'm so sorry,' he said to the salesman, 'We'd gone into the Co-op for a few bits and when I turned round she'd gone. I went home, but of course she wasn't there.' He turned to his wife, 'how did you get here this time?'

'This man brought me. He likes the yellow car too.'

A police car pulled up behind Richie's. Out of it got the two police officers who had dealt with him at the charity shop, just twenty four hours previously.

'What is it this time, Sir? Richard isn't it? This lady has been reported as a missing and vulnerable person, why have you brought her down here?'

Richie explained as well as he could. The explanation sounded distinctly the same as the one the officers had heard yesterday morning: he was only trying to help.

'Of course you were, Sir. You seem always to be trying to help, and yet things go wrong. Mr Cooper will take his wife home now, and I suggest that you go home too.

And we'd really rather not be called out because of your *help* again, Sir.' He made inverted commas with his fingers in the air, 'even if you do have a heart of gold.'

The Call of the Cereal

Lindsay liked to think that she was not easily influenced by adverts. She and her husband knew which products and brands they preferred, and they stuck to them. But this time, this time something was different.

It wasn't an all-singing, all-dancing advert upon which masses of money had been spent. Just a brief ad that was shown in the middle of a TV quiz programme that she was watching. The setting was a kitchen, considerably larger and smarter than their own, with a central, scrubbed wooden table at which sat a woman of about Lindsay's age. She didn't look like Lindsay did at breakfast-time though. This smiling woman was wearing white – it could have been a white blouse and white trousers; it certainly wasn't nightwear, which is what Lindsay often wore at the breakfast table.

The woman's hair was stylishly coiffed and

she was immaculately made up. She seemed to be seamlessly shepherding several children through the early-morning rituals of packing their bags for school, wiping the mouth of a youngster in a high-chair, and feeding them all a healthy breakfast. The kitchen itself looked like something out of *Homes and Gardens* magazine. And all the time she was smiling.

As the older children disappeared from shot the camera focused on the little one, also dressed in white, an immaculate sleepsuit in spite of the breakfast and wearing no bib, playing happily. It then panned to the woman who, still smiling, poured herself a bowl of Frosted Flakes, and topped it with milk from a pristine fridge. She continued to smile as she ate, and to Lindsay that suddenly looked like a very appealing breakfast.

Usually a slice of toast constituted her breakfast if she was lucky; eaten as often as not, on the way to the car, and she didn't even have children to give her an excuse for the regular morning chaos. Nevertheless, the advertising message had worked, and the next time Lindsay was placing her supermarket order she added on Frosted Flakes, just the smallest pack available. She had no illusions that this was just a fad and would quickly be satisfied. When it arrived it seemed to be the biggest pack of Frosted Flakes she had ever seen! They had to rearrange the contents of the dried food cupboard in order for it to fit. Even so it had to be laid on its side.

She was quite correct about the yearning being easily extinguished. The following morning she poured herself a bowl and added milk, just like in the advert. Then her husband shouted about his football boots, which he couldn't find, and Lindsay herself remembered that she was supposed to have read a report for a meeting first thing that morning and so, by the time she was able to lift the first spoonful, the breakfast offering was a sickeningly sweet and soggy mess. It tasted as bad as it looked. Either she had misremembered or maybe the recipe had changed, or her taste buds had. She forced down most of it, before dashing out to work. The following morning she tried a different tack; not adding cold milk until she was absolutely ready to eat. This was better, but still disappointing and she didn't bother again.

She now had the best part of 720 grams of Frosted Flakes and no idea what to do with them. Nobody in the family was interested in eating them, and she knew from past experience that the food banks and food collection points would, understandably, not take anything where the seal had been broken.

At last an idea came to her. She would try just one more bowl, and if it still didn't live up to expectations, then she would take it round to her friend's house. This friend was a keen baker, and would use the contents of the Frosted Flakes packet to either make or decorate some of the many cakes she sold to raise funds for charity.

So she attempted her third bowl of the Frosted Flakes, but after a mouthful or two of the sweet cereal she wanted to gag, and suddenly felt unpleasantly hot and sticky, almost as if she was going to pass out. She made a dash from the kitchen, and reached the bathroom just in time. For Goodness' sake – this used to be her favourite breakfast as a child.

Her mother phoned that lunchtime, and Lindsay told her about the effect the Frosted Flakes had had on her. There was a significant pause.

'Look Lindsay, I'm not saying it's the same, but when I was first expecting you one of the things that I just couldn't stomach was breakfast cereal. I had three months or so when my first meal of every day was lunch. Then, suddenly, I was back to being able to eat anything again. Except oranges and coffee, I went right off oranges and coffee too.'

Expecting? It was one thing that Lindsay hadn't even thought about. What if she was expecting? What if she was reacting the same way her mum had done all those years ago? Had her body really been saying to her 'Look, there's something you should realise – talk to your mum'?

Perhaps so, because within a matter of a few weeks it was indeed confirmed that Lindsay was pregnant. Within a couple of months she once again had the craving for Frosted Flakes that had started her journey, and a 720 gram box disappeared in short order, as did the next box.

Her husband came and stood behind her, his hands on her shoulders. 'Are you enjoying those? It certainly looks like it.'

'I am,' she said, 'They're Gr-r-reat!'

Neighbours

The neighbours seemed rather strange to Thomas, different somehow, a religious sect of some sort his mother had said. She had gone on to explain a sect as a sort of breakaway religion and said that they were called Plymouth Brethren.
They had moved in next door, Mum, Dad and two children, one little more than a toddler, the other about Thomas's age. Not that he ever got to play with them – their lives were very different. They seemed to Thomas to live by the sequences of the moon, or the sun or some such, not by the clock anyway. The clock after all was only standardised to make life easier for train travellers as late as the mid-1800s. Thomas had learned about that at school, and it made a sort of sense. Before that, people lived their life by the seasons and the cycles of the light.
The Plymouth Brethren family seemed hardly ever to have their windows closed and so it was

impossible for Thomas to ignore their early morning singing. This was the children you understand, blasting out hymns such as *Jesus wants me for a Sunbeam* and so on, from dawn onwards, which is pretty early in the UK summer.

His bedroom window overlooked the side of the next door house, which was detached, as was the one where Thomas and his family lived. He learned later that Brethren are not allowed to live anywhere with shared walls, which seemed bizarre to him. It meant no flats and no terraced houses. Children would live in their parents' detached house until they married and had a detached house of their own. This necessarily meant that they could not attend university, and live in communal accommodation. That was all stuff he looked up much later.

When the lights were on, he could see from his bedroom window right into their kitchen, and what a revelation that was! This was in the nineteen sixties, and the kitchen contained every possible modern convenience: an electric mixer, an automatic washing machine, a dishwasher and a deep freeze. These latter two Thomas's mother had believed to be new-fangled goods only available to businesses such as restaurants.

It seemed very odd even to Thomas's young mind, that in spite of all these state-of-the-art gadgets and aids to domestic life, they had no television at all and a radio that, so his mother said, was only used to keep up to date with current affairs, never for entertainment, and it was forbidden to the children.

Another aspect of Thomas's life forbidden to Plymouth Brethren was pets. It seemed odd to a boy growing up in a family who had always kept a dog, that this was seen as unacceptable.

It cannot be said that young Thomas had much interest in the family next door. To reach their house, such was the shape of the cul-de-sac where both families lived, it was necessary to first pass Thomas's corner house. He, on the other hand, had no reason at all to go to go round that corner into the head of the cul-de-sac, and so their lives continued on their separate journeys.

*

When he was a teenager, Thomas's life fell apart. Just home from school one day he opened the door to two men, one of whom his mother, coming up behind him from the kitchen, clearly recognised as a work colleague of his dad. There was no easy way for the two men to share their news. Coming out of work that afternoon his dad had suffered a fatal heart attack. He would not be coming home again, ever.

The early evening passed for Thomas in a blur. People came and went, the vicar, the doctor, neighbours and friends, but one of the first to come to the door was the lady who lived next door. Thomas didn't even know her name or how to address her. He opened the door wide for her to come in, but she remained on the step. In her hands she held a casserole dish containing a meal that made Thomas's stomach rumble as he realised that he had eaten nothing for hours.

Attached to the top of the covered dish was a note about the temperature and length of time for which it should be reheated.

'Please tell your mother how sorry we are to hear of your loss,' she said, and then something which surprised Thomas.

'Tell her to please keep the dish. Our religion does not allow us to share food preparation with people who do not share our beliefs, and so occasionally I buy a few dishes to pass on to people who need them. If she would not want to keep it herself, then please suggest that she passes it on to someone who may.' Many years later Thomas was to read about the charitable spirit that was typical of the Brethren. Certainly this woman seemed an example of that.

This was born out later in the evening when there was another knock at the door. This time it was the man of the house from next door and Thomas's mother answered it herself. He opened by echoing his wife's expression of regret, but he had more to say.

'I know this will be a very difficult time for you, for all sorts of reasons. I particularly know that in financial terms it can be harrowing. You may not realise that your husband's bank account will immediately be frozen, until any will can be processed and funds made available. I would like to reassure you that until that is the case, and you can establish exactly what your financial situation is, I will happily tide you over if you are stuck for funds.'

Thomas's mother went to object, but he had more to say.

'I'm not talking in a professional capacity here. I'm talking about helping out a near neighbour who is going through a difficult time. Please, there is so little that any of us can do to feel that we are helping in some way, so do call on us if you need to.'

With that he was gone. Back to his strange, different, detached world, but leaving behind him a smidgeon of faith in the goodness of humanity and hope for the future.

A Stitch in Time

Well! There I was just enjoying the day to day routine with my woman, when suddenly: Oof! Did you hear that clunk? That's not a good sign. It was really painful and now my foot is stuck! Totally stuck! I knew this would happen, I just knew it, but was I consulted? Of course not! These women, they think they know it all and just go happily on, never asking advice until something goes wrong – like this.

I could have explained that, although I may seem tough, my working mechanism is as delicate as a little flower, and I'm not getting any younger. I'm nearly sixty and I need nurturing and looking after, not dumping on the windowsill and being left there untouched for several years, then expected to perform at will. I should be cossetted and protected. I even have a special cover that is designed to keep the dust, fluff and dirt off my innards. But the clips on the cover broke years ago, and I've been badly treated, left for months on end in the spare room, until I get dragged down to the dining table every now and then and expected to perform like a Formula One car.

Which is what I have done so far, but now it's all gone wrong, and I'm thoroughly stuck. I can't move this foot forwards or backwards, and she's trying all sorts to make it happen. She's got the oil can out and at least it's the proper stuff, meant for machinery like mine, although goodness only knows how long she's had it.

I'm not sure what she's thinking, but if she puts oil anywhere near me while I'm stuck in this position, then there are going to be even more problems. I'm stuck with my foot on the floor or, I should say, on the throat plate. And between my foot and the plate is the pair of curtains we are making together. Or should I say, we were making together until my nether regions seized up.

I don't know exactly what's happened, but the fabric is wedged securely, even though she's tugged and tugged and managed to get my pressure foot up in the air a bit, and boy did that hurt! Something down below called the feed dogs are like wheels with cogs and are supposed to ease the fabric along bit by bit, while I hold it steady and the needle does her work, the up and down bit that I love to watch. Sometimes, on a long stretch like these full length curtains, it nearly sends me to sleep, it's so therapeutic.

Oh my days! What is she doing now? The woman's got the cutting out scissors in her hand. They are enormous! Oh phew, I thought she was going to gouge at me with them, but she's cut along the edge of the fabric and then got the nail scissors and is trying to snip right up to the bit where it's stuck. It's not really working though and now she's having a root round in her sewing box for another weapon. Well, I say her sewing box; it's actually a white hat box that she fastened some pretty ribbon to, so it looks a bit smarter. It's a real Aladdin's Cave and she keeps pulling out all this stuff.

I've no idea what she's looking for, but she's laid to one side a packet of needles and some tailors' chalk. Now she's looking triumphant and she's brought out . . . a crochet hook! What on earth is she going to do with that? Nothing painful I hope. NOW SHE'S COMING AT ME WITH A KNITTING NEEDLE, OH HELP! WHAT'S SHE GOING TO DO? Thankfully it was too large a gauge to fit between me and the throat plate, but it did tickle a bit. I could do with a good scratch now.

That hatbox is full to overflowing with stuff. You see, I'm not the only one who does sewing and suchlike round here. We have crochet materials as I've said; she's made herself a beautiful crochet jacket, but I wasn't involved in that. Then she also does cross-stitch, but again leaves me out. And the knitting – there are all these patterns, and all this wool. Honestly, a fine-tuned machine like I am could be insulted. Although obviously at the moment I'm not fine-tuned at all am I? Otherwise I wouldn't be stuck like this, and it's so embarrassing.

She's having to dig deep, there's fabric and wool everywhere. Fat quarters that she's going to quilt, one day; wool for another cardigan. The last one she crocheted is gorgeous, but I would like to have been involved.

After a good deal of prodding and poking, she eventually released the curtain we'd been working on for an hour. I think she'll have to remake the seams, and the whole lot will be a bit narrower, she's had to cut that much away. I do feel a bit more comfortable now, although it involved her prodding at me with a stitch unpicker, and the curtain looks a right mess where she cut it.

That was a while ago now, and I had been dumped on the floor, when in came an alternative sewing machine! How very rude. This one was electric, with a German name, and state of the art. It looks very sophisticated compared with my straightforward self; does this mean I'm being left on the shelf. Has this new machine taken over? She struggled with the new one over several evenings, trying it on this bit of fabric and that, but I think she had used me for so many years that it didn't come easily and eventually she gave up in disgust. It seems to have disappeared now, I think she's pushed it in the spare room out of the way. I heard her on the phone, asking someone if she could hang onto it for a while.

She got on the internet and talked to someone about mending me. I hope that the person was told her I'd be fine were it not for her neglect. I have my pride. Anyway I spent six days in the Singer repair shop, and now I feel raring to go. The repairman said that I should be treated gently and he's sold her a plastic cover to protect me. It's quite cosy actually and he's worked wonders on my insides. He said that there is some wear understandably, given my age – by which I'm sure he means my experience.

Whilst I was away at the shop, it seems that

the sewing machine my woman had borrowed, she used to try and get the curtains finished.

I heard her say later that she was really confused by it because it wasn't a Singer like me, It was a serious dressmaker that she borrowed it from, and the machine is a fancy German one. Quite a simple soul my woman is, and a creature of habit. She's used a few Singers over the years and said she couldn't cope with threading the needle in a different direction, front to back rather than left to right. Priming the feeds was very different too, and I suppose we all feel happier with what we know. All Singer sewing machines have been roughly the same for years, and to people who use them regularly, like my woman, it becomes almost automatic, the threading and preparing to sew.

Anyway, I'm home now and here we are, back in business. Now if you'll excuse me I need to get back to work. The German machine totally defeated her and she abandoned the project and just returned the German, with thanks, to its owner.

Now, once again, she needs me. Those curtains aren't going to finish themselves.

Chain Gang

The training day was to be held in Croydon, about thirty miles from Beth's home, and not an area she knew well. She had been told that parking would not be a problem; there was a notice enclosed with the day's itinerary, which was to be displayed on her windscreen, and then parking would be free as long as she used the west section of the car park. She decided to get there early, in order to find her way about. It seemed from the map like a huge complex, she would surely be able to grab a coffee somewhere before the first session commenced. Caffeine may help her stay awake. These sessions were not known for their excitement.

She was in plenty of time, and after a quick coffee went for a wander around an indoor market, adjacent to the west end of the car park. And there she saw it.

They had been looking for months for a small cupboard suitable for the hall, but had only been able to find ones that would either project too far into the narrow space, were far too wide for the gap, or were simply open shelving. What they wanted was somewhere to store, hidden from view, essentials like outdoor shoes, gloves, hats, the dog lead and other such paraphernalia.

And here, in this indoor market, miles from home was the perfect item. There seemed to be no-one about, but a stallholder from the next stall saw her interest and wandered over.

'Handy size, isn't it?' she produced a tape measure without being asked, twenty-six inches wide, and . . . just under twelve inches deep. Ideal for a hallway or a little corner. There's the drawer at the top, and inside the lower cupboard is a shelf. Very useful bit of kit, and see the price. I think it's very reasonable. I was quite tempted myself to be honest.'

'You don't need to sell it to me,' Beth told her, 'I'm sold. I'm just a bit concerned about getting it in my car.' She indicated the small hatchback twenty yards away.

'Oh, we can lift it between us I think, don't you?' And they did, laying it flat in the boot.

'You were lucky to catch me,' the woman said. 'I'm Mary, I'm only here helping my daughter to set up her stall this morning, then I'll be on my way. I'll put your money here in his till, and leave a note for Bob, although with the money there, and the cupboard gone, he could probably work it out for himself.'

*

As Beth had expected, the day dragged. When they broke for lunch she wondered whether to go over herself, and thank the stallholder Bob, but decided against it. It was the mother of the neighbouring stallholder who had done all the work, even lifting it into the car by herself as soon as Beth had opened the hatch.

She drove home, and as usual her husband followed a few minutes later. He lifted the cupboard out of her car and into the hall, admired the purchase and then opened the drawer.

'What's with the chains?' he asked.

'Sorry?' Beth came out of the kitchen, 'Oh my! I hadn't opened the drawer. I don't think those should have been left in there do you?'

Opening it had revealed a length of heavy-duty chain, and a hefty padlock. 'We'll have to return these. Do you know the name of the stall where you bought them?'

'Bob,' she told him, 'Oh but that's not going to find him is it? Wait a minute, I have a receipt.'

Digging deep in her handbag, she found the crumpled receipt that the woman Mary had given her, 'Bob's Bits and Bobs,' she read out, 'There's a mobile number.'

She rang the number and it was Bob that answered. 'Thank goodness,' he said, then when he asked where she lived, 'I live not far from there. I'd contacted Mary, but she could only tell me that you drove a blue car – not very helpful. It'll not be till about nine o'clock though. Is that okay?'

Of course it was okay. The alternative was Beth having to make a special trip back to Croydon at some time, just to return the chain and lock.

It was ten past nine when Bob knocked on the door. 'Sorry it's so late,' he said, 'Normally I lock up my stall and leave at about six, but I had to hang on till the outer doors to the market centre were closed and locked at eight. I couldn't leave the unit unsecured. Mary's a kind soul. I think deep down she'd love to work on the market. She's always willing to lend a hand, but of course she'd have no way of knowing that I keep my padlock and chain tucked inside one of the pieces of furniture during the day. It's safer there than just left out on the table where my till is.'

Beth thanked him, both for the cupboard, which he agreed looked good in its new home, and for coming over to collect the chain and padlock, saving her a journey.

'I don't know where I'll put these now. Perhaps I should have kept this little cupboard,' he said, 'instead of selling it.'

'Sorry Bob, too late now.' Beth smiled at him, 'but do yourself a favour. Make sure that Mary knows where you've hidden these in future, so she doesn't sell them again.'

Santa's Shoes

It was the afternoon of Christmas Eve. Grannie Millie sat in the corner chair as the chaos raged around her. The Christmas tree was decorated and took pride of place in the front window, the blinds left open so that passers-by could see it. Eight small children and two teenagers had joined their parents in being invited to the Christmas Eve party, in the hope of tiring the children out sufficiently for the parents to get a lie-in beyond the crack of dawn next day.

So far the party had gone swimmingly. They had eaten their tea and played games; and chased the dog until he had taken himself off to bed for a bit of peace. Now there were sidelong glances between the adults, something was going to happen.

Only one of the children, Daisy, had asked Grannie Millie why she had come on her own. Where was Grandad Wilf? They were all a little concerned about Daisy; she was very close to the Grandad, spending a lot of time with him. Her older sister was sworn to secrecy, but there was a very real fear that Grandad Wilf's identity would be spotted by his precocious little granddaughter. If this happened, she would also be spoiling the surprise for all the local children. Grannie Millie had explained to her that Grandad was tired and having a bit of a lie-down; he may join them later.

Suddenly the sound of children playing could not drown out another sound from the street; the monotonous sound of a large vehicle reversing down the narrow avenue. Some of the children dashed to the front window and peered out. The flashing lights could be seen on top of a large flatbed truck that had stopped outside the door. The yellow livery and flashing lights showed it to be a breakdown recovery vehicle. One of the children shouted, 'Is it Santa? Has Santa come? He's coming tonight, is he here?'

'Yeah, that's his sleigh,' said another and excited children bounced up and down in the window, as the massive AA truck manoeuvred into a space down the road.

Daisy's mother made a hurried phone call to her dad Wilf, who lived opposite, 'You'd better come over as soon as you can, please. The children are all assuming that the AA lorry outside is your sleigh!'

Meanwhile, the driver of the flatbed was waved around to the back door, where Daisy's father explained to his old friend Pete, who worked for the vehicle recovery service, that the children were expecting a visitor and assumed that this was how he had made his arrival.

Pete joined the party, and a few minutes later

there was a 'Ho!Ho!Ho!' and the jingling of bells to be heard outside. Daisy's mum went to the door and let in the suitably attired Santa. He carried a sack of presents for the children and a raucous half hour followed, with children listening for their names to be called, then exploding with happiness as they received a gift from the big man. There were bubble guns, dressing dolls and colouring books; drawing pads and pencils, puzzles and games, and even a cowboy hat for one little boy. For the teenagers were hair bobbles and make-up and a conspiratorial wink.

With all the presents distributed, Santa wished them all goodbye and a Merry Christmas, telling them all to be good and settle down to sleep when their Mummies and Daddies told them to. His exit was followed quickly by Pete. He had only called in because he had been delivering a broken-down car to the next street, and he needed to get back to work, as well as moving *Santa's sleigh* out of sight before the children were taken home. Within a few minutes Grandad Wilf joined them, saying that he had had a lovely rest and would now like to join in the party.
Daisy was disappointed that he had not come across earlier. 'Where were you Grandad Wilf? You should have come before. Didn't you hear the bells jingling? That was Santa's sleigh with the lights and he brought me a present, look.' The other children joined in, until Grandad Wilf, suitably primed with a drink, had admired all the presents.
When all the others had gone home a sleepy Daisy sat on her Grannie's knee.
'Did you like seeing Santa Claus?'

'Yes, and do you know what, Grannie?' She looked down to the floor, 'Santa wears the exact same shoes as Grandad Wilf.'

The Heist

The car park belonged to the cinema in a rundown area of the city. It was full of potholes and not well lit. People tended to park as near to the cinema building as they could, where there was some illumination, but the bottom end of the plot could not be seen from the main road, nor from the front of the cinema. It dropped away quite steeply, and abutted the backs of units under the arches supporting the railway line. These units were accessed from the other side of the railway, so this bit was seldom visited and was pitch dark and, after heavy rain, was frequently flooded. Even from a passing train, someone would need to be hanging out of the window and looking down, in order to see anything happening. That area of the car park only tended to get used when the film showing was very popular and the car park completely full. That was the situation on the evening in this story. Every single parking space was occupied.

For the purposes of Ricky and his friends the car park was ideal. They had equipped a van with old engines for upmarket makes and models of car. They also had a second vehicle, a pickup with lifting gear, which would not join them at the car park until some fifteen or twenty minutes into the main feature of the evening, by which time they knew that the audience would be settled inside for some two or two and a half hours. Sometimes it was very disappointing because the gang couldn't do anything, with no suitable cars having been parked up, but nearly always there was at least one hit. One of the gang, Wayne, was appointed as lookout. No uniform and no booth of course, but he kept a roll of raffle tickets, and would hand them to punters who specifically asked him to keep an eye on their car. He did a nice line in tips too, which he saw no need to share with the other members of the gang or anybody else.

Once the truck with lifting gear arrived at the car park if any punters did arrive late, they would simply assume that someone had broken down and sent for a breakdown truck. This version of events would be confirmed by Ricky and the gang if they were ever challenged, but they never were. What was actually happening was that the team was lifting out the engines from upmarket, newish cars in the car park. These were then replaced by engines from the same or similar models, but older, maybe less powerful, certainly in less good condition. For example, the engine from a year old, top-of-the-range 1800cc model, might be substituted by the engine from a six-year old 1000cc version of the same car.

The car owners who felt their car was running

a little rough, would find out either at its next service or when they checked it out at their garage, or when it broke down that a substitution had been made. The gang was careful to use engines that were in reasonable condition, and they took pride in servicing them beforehand, so that there would hopefully be some time lapse before the owner realised that there was a problem and took it to a professional, who would explain that this was not the engine that had started life in this car. The gang members' plan was that by then, sufficient time would have passed so that the owner would not make a link with their cinema visit weeks or maybe months before.

For several years the gang generated a steady trade in second hand, nearly-new, high-spec engines, selling them on to less scrupulous back-street garages, sometimes stealing a particular model to order. It worked; it worked like a dream. Until one evening it didn't.

One couple left the cinema early. Ricky was never quite sure whether they hadn't enjoyed the film or one of them was feeling unwell. Whatever the reason, this couple approached their car at the bottom end of the car park, and the gang members were caught red-handed. Their car engine had been winched out, and the substitute was ready to go in.

The police found two other engines in the gang's van, both of which had also been destined to swap before the film finished, as well as one newer engine that had been lifted from a car already. Investigation around local garages, especially of the more expensive manufacturers, found that a number of anomalies had already been reported as suspicious in the past eighteen months, and now enquiries with the individuals concerned, all produced confirmation of attendance at that same cinema. Several of the people involved were able to pick Ricky and Wayne, as well as other gang members, out of a line-up.

The cinema is long gone now, and in its place stands a prestigious concert hall, with a well-lit and fully patrolled car park. Other vulnerable cinemas took heed of the press coverage and upgraded their facilities. Ricky, Wayne and the gang spent some time in prison, their mugshots posted for years afterwards on the noticeboards of police stations, cinemas and garages in the area.

Weather, Not Seasons

The gift was special; personal. There was no opportunity in those days to order such personalised gifts on line, sit at home and simply wait for it to be delivered, and so Karen took a bus into town, and walked down to the shop she had identified, to collect the item she had ordered, a carved wooden plaque into interlocking letters that would spell out the baby's name, Emmeline. It was not a name that she herself would ever have chosen, but often babies seemed to grow into their names so she believed. Time would tell.

The plaque was lovely. It comprised different woods, so the colours were more vibrant than she expected, and the hook on the back, by which it could be fixed to a little one's bedroom door, could be removed at a later date maybe, to turn it into a jigsaw for baby Emmeline to play with as she grew older.

Back at the bus stop, Karen was relieved that

she had brought a plastic carrier bag to protect the plaque, as it had begun to rain. The temperature had dropped too, as it so often does in the United Kingdom when the rain comes in. She noticed another woman sit on the other end of the seat in the bus shelter, a woman with jet black hair, and suntanned skin.

After a few moments the woman spoke, 'Is cold,' she said, rubbing her hands on her upper arms.

Karen smiled, there seemed little to say. The woman continued, 'I am disappoint that it is cold and wet. Tomorrow I go to – err – she searched for the word, a wedding of my friends. Will be horrible I think the weather.'

'Where are you from,' Karen wanted to know.

'I am from Bologna, in Italia. Is beautiful and the summer is warm and is sunshine.'

'It's hard to explain,' Karen said to her, 'Here in the UK the weather changes very quickly. It can be warm and sunny one minute, then the clouds come in, the temperature drops and it feels much less pleasant.'

'I see this morning,' the woman, 'In one minute the weather it change, and is like winter now, but is July.'

'In Bologna,' Karen laboured on, 'you have seasons, so in spring the weather gets warmer, then in summer it is nearly always hot and dry, then in the autumn it gets cooler and there is a bit of rain.'

'A bit of rain, yes,' the woman looked skywards as the rain increased. Here is bus now.'

They sat together on the bus. 'You see,' Karen continued, 'here in the UK we have seasons, but more in name only, we can get a really hot morning, then the weather changes and the afternoon can be quite cold.'

'Is this why you always talk about it here? Is always different?'

'Yes,' Karen got ready to get off the bus as her stop loomed, 'where is the wedding you are going to?'

'Is about four kilometres, over there I think,' she waved her arm.

'And what time is the ceremony tomorrow?'

'Is at the church at one o'clock and a half, how you say? Half past one?'

'That's right,' Karen smiled at her. 'Tomorrow at half past one, I will check the weather and think of you. Hopefully it will be dry and the sun will be shining.'

The following morning, Karen dressed carefully, she had a short sleeved dress for the Christening, but took a cardigan in the car with her, along with her umbrella and the carefully wrapped present.

After the short church service they went back to her friend's house for lunch. Emmeline's father fired up the barbecue in the back garden. At half past one Karen was finding it too hot in the sun and retired to the shade of the kitchen. She raised a glass of champagne to the lady from Bologna whom she had met the previous day, hoping that she too was enjoying her celebration in the UK sunshine.

Percy

Garden Centres were in their infancy, a development of the plant nurseries that had gone before. It seems strange looking back, but what is now a well-known chain of garden centres began in the clearing in a corner of farmland with a much-patched polytunnel and a newly installed ice cream fridge. The fridge was very popular over that hot summer of 1955, and was augmented by a couple of chairs and tables – the beginning of the growth phenomenon.

The three children were taken there regularly. Mother was a keen gardener, and she loved rummaging around in the earth of the many plant pots. The children became bored but there were two highlights of any summer visits. It was during their second visit there that, bored as ever, they spotted the newly installed Wall's refrigerator. The range of options was limited and stock had quickly run low, but they were each treated to an ice cream of their choice.

The popularity of the garden centre grew incredibly quickly. More and more families had cars, owned their own homes and wanted to stamp their individuality on their gardens, even if that individuality was the same as that of so many other people.

I heard a story that you could drive down a road, and immediately know which was the nearest garden centre, by the range of plants in all the front gardens. Garden shows sprang up across the country, and garden centres diversified into restaurants, fancy goods sales, and pets.

A heated fish tank now took pride of place in the centre of the pet supply area. A tank on legs, bringing it up to just the right height for small children. On the side of the tank was a hand-written sign *This is Percy the Puffer Fish. Please do not bang on the glass.* The children and their mother looked up puffer fish in the dictionary. The OED refers to it also as a globe-fish and that is defined as any fish that can blow itself up into a near-sphere, presumably to scare off potential predators by its size.

The trips to the garden centre became much more pleasurable for the children. Each time they visited they would dash to Percy's tank and see how much he had grown. The lady at the counter assured them that he would not grow much bigger and that he has plenty of room in the tank. They wanted to know whether he was lonely on his own, and were told that he was not very friendly to other fish, but he liked all the children that came to visit and talk to him. The three youngsters especially liked to be there at three o'clock in the afternoon, when Percy was fed and they could watch him bob up to the surface to grab the fish food flakes, before going right down to the floor of the tank to vacuum up those bits that he had missed.

Then one day they arrived at the garden centre to find an unexpected change. Percy was not there. A sign, written in very grown-up writing that the three could not read, was pinned high on the wall where his tank had stood, and where now a pile of tinned dog food was displayed. No doubt the idea was that parents could read the sign for themselves, and decide how much, and what information to pass on to their children.

The sign read:

Sadly Percy the Puffer Fish is no longer with us. Overnight at the weekend the thermostat on his tank broke and unfortunately the water became too hot for Percy to live in. You may wish to tell your children that happily he has gone to live elsewhere. Please let them know that he loved all the visitors that came to see him and hopes that you all enjoy looking at the other fish in the cool tanks, and that you will still come to visit us and enjoy our ice-cream.

Poor Percy. It was a gentle way of saying that the thermostat had broken, and they had, quite unintentionally, cooked him!

David's Inheritance

The two girls, Elsie and Brenda, sat next to each other on a double desk in primary school. The teacher had decreed that the new intake should sit in alphabetical order according to the children's surnames, so that she might get to know who was who from these thirty two tiny strangers as quickly as possible. It is a truth that all teachers know, that the first children you get to know are the troublesome ones; after that there are the brightest or best-behaved

those who make a weary teacher remember why she chose that as her profession. The last names to be learned are of the vast cohort that come in the middle, and it is in this group that these two girls fell. Webster, their surname was and the families had established that they were of no relationship whatsoever.

The two kept in touch throughout their school years and both went, aged fourteen into employment at the biscuit factory, one of the few unskilled options for the girls of the town. Elsie married an up-and-coming young businessman and subsequently had two sons. The romantic path of Brenda's life was rather less smooth. It was not until Elsie's family was complete that she found happiness in marriage, although sadly they were not blessed with the patter of tiny feet. After a number of years Brenda and Peter adopted a young, troubled boy through an official agency attached to their place of worship. His name was David.

Initially Elsie's younger boy Gilbert and Brenda's were close, but it soon became evident to Elsie that there was a malicious side to young David, something that she didn't want her boys either to copy, nor to suffer from. On a couple of occasions she saw David as he made his way home from school and he was clearly taunting and bullying smaller boys; not necessarily younger boys, as right from the time of his adoption he was a big strong lad who as an adult went on to top out at six foot four inches tall.

Fortunately for Elsie the boys' futures diverged on leaving school. Gilbert went away to university. David was very keen to join the police force, but his parents strongly objected. At sixteen years of age, with no other means of support he had little choice but to bow to their wishes. He went therefore to work in Peter's office, hated it and as soon as he had acquired a sufficient nest egg he moved out, leaving them no forwarding address and breaking his adoptive parents' hearts.

The Webster families remained friends, first as a foursome, subsequently the two widows. By the time Brenda died her friend was an old woman, and to her surprise she found that her younger son Gilbert had been named as executor to Brenda's will. Less surprising was that the sole beneficiary was Brenda's adopted son David Webster. So far, so good; except that no members of either family had seen or heard of David for over three decades. These days a post on social media may well have been all it took, but at that time social media was in its infancy. Gilbert did try one school-based site, Friends Reunited, to see if any friends, old or recent, could put him in touch with David, but again there was no response.

Gilbert's next approach was to the Citizens' Advice Bureau, who offered a half hour interview with a solicitor at no charge. He was told something that he didn't know – he had a responsibility only to explore all *reasonable* avenues to find David. The solicitor suggested approaching the church involved in the adoption, and perhaps to advertise in the newspapers.

The adoption agency involved in David's placement had closed down, and the only remaining records were his adoption certificate, a facsimile of which Gilbert had found in his Aunty Brenda's effects. He placed adverts in a national newspaper for three successive weeks, trying to entice David to enquire about something that *may be to his benefit*, but again he waited in vain for a response.

On the advice of a friend he approached the Salvation Army, who tried to track down David Webster but without success. Gilbert also tried their old school to see if anyone there knew of his whereabouts. It was a long shot. David had left school as soon as he could at sixteen and their records didn't go back that far. One of the oldest of the teachers was able to say that David had applied for employment way back then at a local wood yard, but had not got the job. Maybe it would be worth Gilbert contacting other similar businesses. Suddenly it all seemed so futile, such a waste of time. Thirty years had passed. David could be anywhere in the world; he could have passed away or he could have applied for his birth details since the law had changed, and maybe was now known under another name altogether. Gilbert couldn't access the records of a third party, so this was a dead end. He had already made a number of phone calls, and paid for the newspaper advertisements. The solicitor had told him that he could claim these expenses back from the estate, but he could see David's fairly modest inheritance being whittled away before he even knew anything about it.

He decided to go again to the Citizens' Advice Bureau. This time it was a different solicitor. He was her last appointment of the session and she was happy to chat. He set out the bare bones of his problem as she listened with her head on one side.

'Have you heard of Jarndyce versus Jarndyce?' she asked him.

'Sounds familiar, it's in a book I think?'

'That's right. Charles Dickens' Bleak House, written in 1852.'

'What does that have to do with me and David?' Gilbert wanted to know.

'It was based on a real life case from about eighteen hundred – Jennens versus Jennens. William Jennens died leaving approximately two million pounds. I think that would be about two billion in today's money. The family took each other to court and it wasn't resolved for over a hundred years.'

'I remember now. In the Dickens story the money runs out before it's resolved.'

'That's right. And the same had happened in the Jennens case. The lawyers continued to proceed out of interest to see how it transpired, long after the money had gone. I would say that you have done everything reasonable to try and track down Mr Webster. Anything more in depth, such as hiring a private investigator, is potentially massively expensive and with no guarantee that you would be any more successful.'

'So what should I do?'

'Donate it to a charity in the name of the late Brenda Webster. That would be a much better use for it.'

And so the following weekend the local animal charity was the grateful recipients of a generous donation of nearly six thousand pounds.

And so to Bed

Are you an adult? Are you in a relationship? If so, at night do you share a bed with your significant other? If so, why? This may seem a controversial question, but hear me out.

I think I'm right in saying that throughout their formative years every child I have ever known has slept in their own bed, usually a bed three feet wide, or maybe two foot six wide when they were very small, or shared bunk beds with a sibling. Most also had the luxury of their own bedroom when they are growing up if they were lucky. So while we are, effectively, undersized human beings, we have a full three foot wide bed in which to spread out and sleep in whatever position we choose. (That's more than ninety centimetres in new money.)

Then we grow up and what happens? We meet someone we chose spend our life with, and not just our waking life, but our sleeping life too, and I would suggest that most couples as adults, instead of giving ourselves plenty of space in which to sleep, opt for half of a conventional double bed to share with a partner. Now, given that a standard double bed is four foot six wide, (one hundred and thirty five centimetres) then we effectively wait until we reach our full size – some of us much larger than others, then eschew a three-foot wide space for one that is just a paltry two foot three inches. Why? Now, I'm no giant, but if I'm sitting up in bed, holding a book then from one elbow to the other already measures more than two foot three!

We don't, I suggest, tend to spend our waking leisure time sitting side by side on an inadequately small sofa. In my experience adults are more likely to sprawl in a chair, with their partner sitting or lying on the sofa, or in an adjacent chair. One may prefer to put their feet up, the other not. Yet we seem to happily retire for the night to a room where we sleep, squashed into a narrower space than we have ever slept in in our lives. It seems crazy, especially if one half of the couple prefers to sleep in, say, the starfish position, or curled up in a ball, in which case they are bound to transgress the imaginary line down the centre of the bed.

Many master bedrooms, particularly modern ones, have no space for anything more generous than a standard double bed. But it's not just the space, although this can be a real problem. Take a situation where one party has always slept with the window open, and has to acclimatise to another warm body taking up what seems to be the limited amount of oxygen in a room where the window is closed. The bedroom door too may be a bone of contention – to close or leave it open. And what of radiators? If one party has always slept with a radiator on in the bedroom, yet the other prefers to sleep in a cool room who decides? It is a domestic minefield.

The bed itself of course, can be a challenge in terms of more than just its size. Finding one to suit the posture and preference of two people, who are potentially very different sizes and of different weight is difficult, to say nothing of the individuals' liking for a hard, medium or soft mattress. One may be accustomed to sleeping in total darkness, with thick, dark curtains blocking the windows if necessary. The other may want the room light and bright, and be happy to see early morning sun peeping through the window. And who decides which side of the bed they sleep on? What if they both have a preference for sleeping near the window, or further away from the window?

This is before we have considered the bedding with which this anomaly is dressed. Pillows are usually bought singly, or in pairs so a choice can be happily made, even if one party prefers a much harder head support than the other, or if one prefers to sleep in a more upright position. But what about the covers?

A duvet will declare its tog rating, but seldom gives the option of flexibility. If one of you is having a heavy duvet then so is the other – whether they like it or not. Blankets are equally inflexible; there is no scope for one party being covered with a blanket, and not the other, and then there are electric blankets. Although these days they can be heated separately in two halves, it is not really possible to heat up just one half of a bed, especially when the body beside you has their side of the electric blanket switched on high, and is getting warmer and warmer.

We have considered heat, light, weight of covers, and how hard the mattress is – all reasonable causes for disagreement, but surely one of the biggest challenges must be where there is a difference in the ability to tolerate noise. Those who like the window open are likely to hear morning birdsong, but also perhaps the less appealing noise of traffic, and maybe that of drunks rolling home from the pub. Closing the window may alleviate these external problems, but if one half of a partnership snores, the noises may well be unavoidable.

We touched on light and the use of curtains, but what of timing? One party may choose to relax in bed by reading a book, which requires adequate light, or by watching television. The other may find these intrusive, and prefer to immediately settle for sleep.

It very much begs the question why? Why do we surrender our previous generous sleeping space in order to spend approximately a third of our adult lifetime in an inadequate space just because it seems to be expected of us? It makes no sense at all.

Good Night.

Acknowledgements

I firstly need to acknowledge the contribution of my daughter, whose interest in British Sign Language triggered the writing of this series of books raising funds the British Deaf Association.

Her interest was mirrored and built upon by her daughter Grace, who became interested to the extent of making BSL her future career and who has completed her degree in BSL and Deaf and now works in supporting the deaf community.

I want to thank members of the book club, Barbara, Clare, Freda, Gayle, Gill, Hilary, Jennifer, Kerry, Liz, Sue B, Sue R, and Sue S, who have tolerated being read to and who have commented, informing changes to some of the stories.

A particular mention goes to Gayle, whose description of her books rolling their eyes when she added to their number inspired Opposites Attract.

Many thanks, as always, to the wonderful and positive Bowen's Book Publicity for highly professional promotional posts.

In the story called The Tree Feller did you find the different tree species hidden in the story? There are seventeen in total. Can you find them all? This is the order in which they are hidden.

Fir, Ash, Aspen, Lilac, Alder, Lime, Poplar Beech, Plane, Sorbus, Yew, Willow, Oak, Maple, Elder, Cedar, Holly

Printed in Great Britain
by Amazon